CASE OF THE

HOBBIT HEIST

J.M. POOLE

Mysteries by J.M. Poole
The Corgi Case Files Series
Available in e-book and paperback

Case of the One-Eyed Tiger
Case of the Fleet-Footed Mummy
Case of the Holiday Hijinks
Case of the Pilfered Pooches
Case of the Muffin Murders
Case of the Chatty Roadrunner
Case of the Highland House Haunting
Case of the Ostentatious Otters
Case of the Dysfunctional Daredevils
Case of the Abandoned Bones
Case of the Great Cranberry Caper
Case of the Shady Shamrock
Case of the Ragin' Cajun
Case of the Missing Marine
Case of the Stuttering Parrot
Case of the Rusty Sword
Case of the Unlucky Emperor
Case of the Ice Cream Crime
Case of the Hobbit Heist

If you enjoy Epic Fantasy,
check out Jeff's other series:
Bakkian Chronicles
Tales of Lentari
Dragons of Andela

CORGI CASE FILES

CASE OF THE

HOBBIT HEIST

BOOK 19

J.M. POOLE

Secret Staircase Books

Case of the Hobbit Heist
Published by Secret Staircase Books, an imprint of
Columbine Publishing Group, LLC
PO Box 416, Angel Fire, NM 87710

Book layout and design by Secret Staircase Books
Corgi illustrations by Igor Zubkov
First trade paperback edition: February, 2024
First e-book edition: February, 2024

* * *

Publisher's Cataloging-in-Publication Data

Poole, J.M.
Case of the Hobbit Heist / by J.M. Poole.
p. cm.
ISBN 978-1649141620 (paperback)
ISBN 978-1649141637 (e-book)

1. Zachary Anderson (Fictitious character)—Fiction. 2. Amateur
sleuth—Fiction. 3. Pet detectives—Fiction. 4. Comic-con events—
Fiction. I. Title

Corgi Case Files Mystery Series : Book 19.
Poole, J.M., Corgi Case Files mysteries.

BISAC : FICTION / Mystery & Detective.

813/.54

For Giliane —

You make me smile in more ways than I thought possible.
Love you always & forever!

Acknowledgements

Thanks go out to my wife, Giliane, for listening to me ramble on and on about possible ideas for stories, scenes, and what I should make the characters do. Many thanks to the members of my Posse, for adding even more spit and polish to the story before it's placed in the readers' hands. This time around, I'd like to give thanks to Posse Members: Mefe, Jason, Louise, Diane, Caryl, Carol, and the rest of my team. I'd also like to give shout-outs to the team of people at my publisher: Marcia Koopmann, Susan Gross, Sandra Anderson, Paula Webb, and Isobel Tamney. Many thanks to all of you who point out ways I can improve myself as a writer. :)

I'd also like to thank my good friend Michael Biehn, and his wife, Jennifer, for agreeing to be in the story. Several of you can actually say you've met a celebrity or two. Not many can say they're friends with them. If you ever have a chance to meet Michael, you'll find that he'll take the time to get to know you and will treat you with respect. He's very down-to-earth, and probably one of the most approachable guys I've ever known.

Finally, I give my thanks to you, the reader, for allowing me to keep the stories about Zack and the dogs going!

A FRAPPIN' CORGI NEVER CEASES TO AMAZE!

FOREWORD

Hello, this is Michael Biehn. Many of you may recognize me from the various roles I've been fortunate to play in a number of movies, such as *Terminator*, *Aliens*, *The Abyss*, *The Rock*, and *Tombstone*, to name a few. What you're about to read is a story from a good friend of mine, Mr. Jeffrey M. Poole. Jeff and I first met back when we both happened to be in the same small city in Arizona at the same time. I had requested help to fix my computer, and he just happened to be a mobile computer tech. A friendship began, and discovering we each had a mutual love of movies, he and I have stayed in contact with one another ever since.

What you're about to read is a story that I could easily see happening in real life. I do attend comic cons, and as is the case with this story, my wife, Jennifer, almost always accompanies me. For us actors, it's a fantastic way to meet the fans. Have I ever brought a prop with me? No, I haven't. And for the record, no, I did not keep the M-41A pulse rifle I used in *Aliens*, even though this story suggests I did. *Case of the Hobbit Heist* is an enjoyable tale about new friendships, two highly entertaining dogs, and a remarkable set of *what if* circumstances. And, if you look closely, you'll be able to spot where Jeff has added some Easter eggs. The story of me looking for a certain grave in a remote, rural area of Arizona? True. Jeff and I learned the hard way that you do *not* go unprepared to any outdoor excursion. Especially without cell service. But, that first time was a learning experience, and we did get better. Didn't find the grave, though.

So, do I really have a website that I submit my own stories to? Yes. And, it's the same one advertised in this book. SettingHistoryStraight.com was created a few years ago as a means to educate others about certain topics history has gotten wrong. You'll find a number of articles about Tombstone, behind the scenes of the movie, and just how badly Hollywood got some facts wrong, along with some of my own personal stories. Again, kudos to Jeff for being the one who made everything happen.

I hope you enjoy the story as much as I did. If you'd like to follow me online, I'm now on Instagram, or you can find me at https://instabio.cc/MichaelBiehn.

Take care, and stay frosty out there!

Michael Biehn

ONE

Living in a huge mansion has its moments. For starters, just trying to find one's significant other when there's more than seventy-five hundred square feet of living space is a chore in itself. Then again, I had no one to blame but myself. After all, I'm the one who picked out the plans for this behemoth. I'm the one who looked at the four-level monstrosity and said, why not?

The master suite was in the northwest corner of the first floor. My darling wife, however, was not. Then again, it wasn't really too difficult to figure out where she could be. After all, from the moment I showed her the secret library I had built just for her, Jillian had worked tirelessly to get everything put in its place. Books, furniture, more books, craft tables, and did I mention books? That woman loves to read more than I do, and I'm the writer in the family.

Oh, I'm sorry. Let me make the formal introductions. My name is Zachary Anderson. Zack, for short. I'm married to a wonderful, beautiful woman by the name of Jillian. She and I haven't been married long, as this is the second marriage for each of us, having both been widowed a few years ago. Neither of us were looking for romance, but we couldn't deny what we felt for each other.

As I mentioned earlier, I'm a writer. I'm known for my, er, *spicy* romance novels, penned under my nom de plume, Chastity Wadsworth. I know what you're thinking. Why write under a female name? Well, when it comes to romance novels, female authors have been known to outperform their male counterparts, so I let my fans and readers think that Chastity is a real person.

Not long ago, I published a book entitled *Heart of Éire*, which was a far cry from my usual fare, this one under a new pseudonym—Jim McGee. That particular book was born from an idea posed by my good friend, a detective on the local police force, as an anniversary present for his wife. Set in Ireland, the story focuses on a single mother doing everything she can to keep her family alive during the great potato famine of the mid-1840's.

I never would have imagined the book could do so well. It rocketed to the top of the charts and, for the first time ever, one of my titles hit the *NY Times Best Seller* list and stayed there for an impressive amount of time. Naturally, my publisher was hungry for more, so they did everything they could to facilitate a sequel. I, for one, wasn't about to undertake the challenge unless I knew the story would be worthy of the original.

Again, I misjudged just how much people enjoyed reading a story which involved the Emerald Isle. *Spirit of Éire* won't be released for another month or two, yet it has already garnered thousands of pre-sales. My publisher gleefully told me that it is tearing up the charts in record time.

Since I'm still talking about me, I should also tell you about another business venture I have, one that I inherited not long after my first wife died. I'm a winery owner in southern Oregon. Lentari Cellars is a local favorite, and when it became known I was the new owner, I made both friends and enemies in the blink of an eye. Friends, in the sense that the locals were eager to see me reopen the winery and get production back on track. The enemies came not that long afterward, accusing me of accepting something that should never have been given to me in the first place. One particular family has tried numerous times to wrest the winery from me, but thankfully, I was too stubborn to allow myself to be intimidated.

The final tidbit I need to pass along has to do with the third job I hold. Are you wondering what other hat I could possibly wear? If it wasn't blatantly obvious, I don't have enough on my plate, then it should be now. Because of my two roommates, I was hired on as a paid consultant for the Pomme Valley police. I'd like to say that I'm the secret weapon the PVPD turns to whenever they need help solving a crime, but that'd be one mother of a lie. No, the police only care about my two dogs.

Sherlock and Watson.

Where do I start with them? Well, I can say that they are probably the most unintimidating dogs you could possibly find. Don't believe me? Look up Pembroke Welsh

Corgis. While the breed may be unfamiliar, I can pretty much guarantee you've seen these dogs before. Take the late Queen of England. They were her favorite choice of furry companions.

Corgis typically have an overall height ranging from between fourteen and seventeen inches, and a weight from twenty-five to thirty pounds (for the males). Females are slightly smaller. Most will have their tails docked at birth, but lately, I've started seeing more of the adorable little low-rider dogs with their tails intact.

Sherlock and Watson are probably the most well-known dogs in southern Oregon. Those two little canines have the ability to sniff out clues relevant to whatever case we happen to be working. No matter how absurd the *corgi clue* might appear, they will always link to the case in some fashion. Every. Single. Time.

That is why the local police department is interested. They couldn't give a fig about the guy holding the leashes. All they see when they look at me is simply the owner of ye almighty detective dogs. But, all kidding aside, I love my two corgis. I couldn't imagine my life without them.

So, let's recap. I'm happily married … to a missing wife. I'm the proud owner of two corgis, who are also mysteriously absent. I hold down a number of jobs, and my dogs are way more famous than I'll ever be. Oh, and I'm currently living in a brand new, way-too-big-for-two-people mansion. Did I leave anything out?

Exiting the northwest wing of the house, I found myself in a two-story foyer. A set of stairs leading to the other floors in my house was on my left, and visible to the right was the vast Grand Salon, a forty-two foot long, twenty-foot-wide chamber situated in the heart of the manor. The salon held a huge fireplace, with enough plush sofas and chairs to comfortably seat twenty people.

I took the stairs and headed down. This was the basement, or as Jillian called it, the ground floor. And, it was my favorite level in the house. Why? That's because the things one could find down here would delight any kid, young or old.

The first thing you see as you emerge onto the ground floor is the large bar and wine counter directly on the right. Now, I'm not a fan of wine in general, but I do know Jillian likes a glass every now and then. Plus, who wouldn't like to sit down for a beer at a bar installed in their own house? Several local brews are on tap, and you'll find a well-stocked wine fridge that'd put a four-star restaurant to shame.

Fighting off the urge to stop for a mug or two, I glanced to the right. Ah, there it is, my pride and joy. The game room. Nearly two dozen classic retro arcade cabinets were arranged back-to-back in the center of the room. Also, situated on two of the perimeter walls was a collection of pinball machines. Thanks to the power of the internet, I was able to track down all my favorites and bring them here. I should also mention that the third wall, on the right, had two nine-foot-long machines that were two feet wide and, at the tallest point, five and a half feet tall. What were they? Two official Skee-Ball cabinets, of course. These weren't the much smaller replicas that were currently for sale, or the new models which were modified for home use. No, these machines came from actual arcades and restaurants that were phasing them out, or else replacing them. I managed to snag a pair of the machines, had them painstakingly restored, and arranged them next to each other in the right-hand alcove. As a matter of fact, Vance, Harry, and I just had a tournament last week. Can I say I won? Nope. I clearly need to practice. Harry took the honors that time around.

Walking past the multiple silent gaming machines, I hesitated. I thought for certain I had just heard a dog bark. Nodding, I continued walking. The sound was coming from my left, and *down*.

I reached the large area directly beneath the grand salon and faced the large video screen, which was currently dark. A fireplace was here, and it had to be about three times the size of the one upstairs. The surround was natural granite, and extended all the way to the ceiling. Installed above the fireplace was a huge flat-panel television.

I knew there was a secret door on the left of the surround, molded ingeniously into the rock face. The door allowed access to the tech room hidden behind the fireplace, thus allowing me access to all of my home theater's electronics, making it easier to service or replace components as necessary. Friends have watched me enter this room on numerous occasions, and each of them thought the idea of a secret room was a blast.

What they didn't know was that on the right side of the fireplace, there was a second door. This one could only be accessed by pressing in on a specific stone. The latch would release, and the door could be pushed open. Stepping through the doorway revealed a brightly lit corridor, leading to a staircase going down.

This was the secret entrance for Jillian's personal library. It was located about twenty feet below the basement and had around four hundred square feet of space. I should also point out there were bookcases lining every wall. I had offered to take a few down and install a TV, but my wife nixed that idea. Then, a few days later, she compromised and had me remove *one* bookcase, which allowed her to install a crafting desk.

This was the area where I had heard the bark. I think Jillian had come down here to relax, and Sherlock and Watson had naturally followed.

"Do you hear that?" I heard Jillian ask. "I do believe your daddy has found us!"

"It took a while," I admitted, as I emerged into her room. "I see that you've got a lot of your books displayed. Good for you! They look great!"

"Come, see what I did with the desk. Look! I have my jewelry-making supplies here, and I have my scrapbooking supplies there. I installed some shelving over there, which holds several of the tools I'll be using to turn all of our sea glass collection into jewelry."

I nodded and sank down into one of the four barrel chairs Jillian had elected to set around her area. Sherlock, my tri-colored boy, jumped down from the chair he had claimed and trotted over to me. He gave my hand a friendly lick before turning to look at my wife. Once Jillian had returned to her chair, Sherlock jumped up onto her lap.

"He's spoiled rotten," I observed with a laugh.

At that exact moment, my red and white corgi appeared in front of me and reared up on her hind legs, which is her way of asking to be picked up.

"Watson! Good to see you, pretty girl."

Watson promptly curled up on my lap. I gave Jillian a shrug.

"Go ahead. Say it."

"I don't need to," Jillian laughed.

"Is Ruby down here?" I asked.

Ruby was the African gray parrot I had unintentionally

inherited after her previous owner passed away. For whatever reason, the little gray bird had become fixated with me, so when it came time to rehoming the talkative parrot, yours truly had been chosen. Oh, well. At least my three animals all got along together.

"She was asleep in her cage earlier," Jillian reported.

"Has to be still asleep, or else I would have heard her. It was way too quiet up there. How long had I been out, anyway?"

"Well, I wanted to let you sleep. I know you had a fretful night last night."

"Yeah, I'm sorry about that. Serves me right, I suppose."

"Really, Zachary. Haven't you told me time and time again how much you hate horror movies, especially with werewolves? And that particular movie, about some tourist in London who changes into one, didn't you say it gave you nightmares?"

"When I was little," I clarified.

"And now?"

"I wanted to prove to myself that I could watch that in our theater and not have it affect me."

Jillian set the book she had been reading on a table next to her. "And?"

"And, it would appear I have a way to go. I still hate werewolves."

"I have something that might brighten up your day," Jillian said, as she reached for her tablet computer. She tapped the screen for a few moments before holding it out to me. "I saw this earlier. I'm surprised they haven't called yet."

"What do you have there?" I asked, as I rose from my

chair and took the tablet. The webpage displayed on the portable computer had me gasping with surprise. "You're kidding. Already? *Spirit of Éire* hasn't been released yet!"

"The number of preorders must be through the roof," Jillian said.

"Wow. I hit the *NY Times Best Seller* list. Again. How cool is that?"

"We should celebrate," Jillian decided. "I think we should have dinner out tonight. Your choice this time."

I looked up. "My choice? And you won't argue about what I choose?"

My wife sighed and offered me a smile. "We're celebrating your accomplishment. You get to choose. All I ask is that we don't have to pull around to a second window to pick up the order."

"Fast food?" I asked, as I rubbed my hands together. "Dost thou thinketh that little-ith of me?"

"Dork," Jillian laughed. "Do you know where you want to go?"

"Oh, the possibilities are endless. I think … I think I might be drunk with power."

My wife giggled. "You're a goofball. So, are you ready for this weekend?"

"The convention? Oh, you bet. I never knew Medford hosted their own comic con."

"Well, they haven't had one in a while," Jillian admitted. "It takes a lot to put one of those on, and even more so to get some recognizable talent to agree to come."

"It'll run through all three days, right? Friday through Sunday?"

Jillian nodded. She reached for something on the table, next to her book. She held up a couple slips of paper. I saw printed information on them, but couldn't make out what it said. A few moments later, I watched her slide those pieces of paper into separate lanyards and then dangle them in front of me.

"Can you guess what I have here?"

"You found the receipts for the air hockey table? Can't imagine why you'd want to preserve them like that."

"No, I … what?"

"What?" I asked, feigning ignorance.

"What did you say?" Jillian asked.

"Hmm? *No comprendo, Señora.*"

"You're lucky I enjoy a good game of air hockey. Anyway, no, these are VIP passes to the Medford comic con."

I straightened in my chair. "You're kidding. For which day?"

"All three," Jillian told me. "You can choose which day you want, or hit all three. It's entirely up to you. Have you ever been to a comic con with a VIP pass strapped around your neck?"

I confirmed I hadn't.

"It's the absolute best. You get priority seating, discounts on merchandise, and are able to meet the celebrities in person instead of standing in line and waiting for an autograph."

I took the tickets and gave my wife a bear hug.

"Thank you so much! Wait, does this mean I'm going to meet …?"

"Mr. Michael Biehn, yes it does."

I'm sure the goofy-looking grin on my face spoke volumes. "He's been in some of my favorite movies."

"I know he has. That's why I did this for you. I thought

you might like to meet him."

"I wonder what he's like in person?" I asked.

"Well, in two days' time, you'll find out. As for me, I'm actually looking forward to seeing what the vendors are carrying. I was serious when I said it before. Your game room needs some mementos. We need to give the space some character."

"And you'll hear no complaints from me. I will admit, it's been years since I've been to one of these. Do they carry anything besides comic books and figurines? That's all I saw at my last convention."

Jillian shrugged. "You should see any number of things, like shirts, hats, mugs, and pretty much anything that can be customized. Personally, I'm hoping to see some decent collectibles."

I turned to Jillian with surprise etched all over my face. "Okay, I knew you were into sci-fi and fantasy movies. But, I didn't know there were any movies out there that interested you so much that you'd want a collectible from it. Can I ask what movies interest you?"

"Well, I do like *Princess Bride*, of course. Then there's *Willow*. And *Star Wars*, naturally."

"They don't typically bring the super-expensive stuff, do they?" I asked. "Like, swords, signed swag, and so on?"

"The larger conventions usually do," Jillian said. "This one is on the smaller side, so I'm thinking probably not. But, that's the fun in looking. You never know what you're going to find."

"I wonder who else will be there," I mused, as I sat back in the chair and studied the tickets Jillian had given me.

"PV has a couple of celebrities living here," Jillian said,

as she picked up her book. "I'll bet we see them there."

This got my attention. "Oh? Like who?"

"Well, for starters, the guy who was in the *Evil Dead* series."

My eyes lit up. "I know who you're talking about! He was in *Army of Darkness,* wasn't he? That movie was hysterical! I had no idea he lived in Pomme Valley. That's so cool!"

"Didn't you know? I could've sworn I've told you before."

I shrugged. "Entirely possible. I have a tendency to zone out whenever I'm working on a story."

"You have a tendency to zone out on me when you're writing," Jillian confirmed, offering me a smile.

"I *was* writing. That makes sense. Okay, I'm not losing it. Wow. I'd love to meet him, too. This is shaping up to be one heck of a weekend!"

If I only knew. Come Sunday, the entire town would be talking about what happened here for months to come, and naturally, my name would be attached to it.

My cell phone rang. One glance at the display had me letting out a heavy sigh.

"Who is it?" Jillian asked.

"MCU. Let's see what my publisher wants this time. Hello? Yes, this is Zack Anderson. Who's this? Well, Ms. Charters, it's nice to meet you, too. What are you …? You're what? Oh? What happened to … hang on a sec. You're going way too fast. You want to what? Oh, now I see why you're speaking as fast as you are."

"What is it?" my wife whispered.

"They want to arrange some promos. Most specifically, a book signing. I … Ms. Charters? No, that wasn't to you, it was to my wife. Now, as you have no doubt been made aware, I'm not too keen on book signings. It's really not my thing. I'd much rather stay home, thank you very much. So … hold it where? Here? In Pomme Valley? Wow, that bit me on the butt, didn't it? Oh, you're good, lady. Hang on, I'm putting you on speaker."

"I'm sorry, Mr. Anderson," a woman's voice was saying, "but I have to admit I did my homework. You're right, I know all about your aversion to public events. That's why we're hoping to arrange something in a small town. Your town, in fact."

"Our friend, Dottie, owns pretty much the largest bookstore in the area, and she has room for no more than a dozen people in her store," I told the publicist. "So, I'm not sure where you think we could have it."

"What about your store, Mrs. Anderson?" the MCU rep innocently asked.

Jillian gave a little start of surprise.

"And what do you know of my store?" my wife asked, leaning forward in her chair. "And how did you know I was here?"

"The audio changed, so I knew I was on speakerphone. Additionally, if you're arranging it so that others can hear the call, that typically means you'd like your significant other to listen in. Therefore, Mrs. Anderson had joined the call."

"You have terrific insight," Jillian observed.

"You have to in this line of work. As I was saying, your store is much larger and is capable of holding many more people inside. And you've hosted events before."

"She really *has* done her homework," I said to Jillian.

"But not thorough enough," Jillian said, shaking her

head. "Ms. Charters, is it?"

"Call me Kathleen. It's Jillian, right?"

"It is. Well, Kathleen, you're right, I do have a store, and it's more than capable of handling a much larger crowd, but I have to ask you something. Do you know what I sell?"

"I thought it was books," Kathleen protested. The sounds of papers rustling could be heard. "It's what I have here."

"Well, you're partially right," Jillian confirmed. "Let me put it another way. What's the *name* of my store? Do you have it there?"

"Let's see. Here it is. It's … oh. I'm so sorry. I totally missed that. You sell cookbooks?"

"It's a specialty kitchen business," Jillian said. "And the events you speak of *were* hosted here, but they were by cookbook authors. I'm not sure Cookbook Nook is the right fit for this."

"May I put you on a brief hold?" Kathleen asked.

"Of course."

"I think their ace in the hole was to find a local business to host this signing," Jillian told me. "However, they underestimated PV's size. They'd have better luck in Medford."

"Mr. and Mrs. Anderson? Are you still with me?"

"We're still here," I reported.

"You're right. MCU would love to have an event in a local store that already has your titles for sale. I can also say MCU is very adamant about getting Mr. Anderson to do a signing. And, from what I can tell, they'll just about agree to anything to make it happen. So, my question for you is, what *will* it take to get this to happen?"

I was drumming my fingers on my armchair. "One of the stipulations I have with MCU is that book signings are, and will forever be, totally optional. I'm sure you know that. New Orleans has soured me on doing any more, so I'm leaning toward a gentle, but firm no. However, I will pass along a message that you can take to your boss."

"And that is?" Kathleen asked. I could hear the eagerness in her voice. She had guessed—correctly—that I was about to offer a compromise.

I looked at my wife and smiled. "Host this signing at Cookbook Nook. If it's at my wife's store, here in my home town, then I'll agree."

"But, your wife's business focuses on the kitchen," Kathleen protested.

"That's my offer," I said. "You'll have to find some way to make it work. I don't know, ship a selection of books to us so that Jillian can offer them in her store. Maybe ..."

"We accept," Kathleen interrupted.

"You agreed to that much too quickly. That means ... say hello, Richard."

There was a pause.

"Hello, Zachary," came the deep rumble of my rep at MCU.

"I usually pick up the hints that you're on the line much faster than that. Man, getting old sucks. How have you been?"

"Good, thanks. You heard Ms. Charters, yes? We agree to your terms."

"That's good to hear. You'll take care of making certain Cookbook Nook has a generous selection of my books?"

"We will, yes."

I spent an additional ten minutes on the phone,

hammering out the details. Additional copies were ordered for Dottie's store, since she owned the actual book store where MCU wanted to host the signing. But, as mentioned earlier, her store is way too small. Jillian therefore agreed to allow Dottie to set up a booth inside Cookbook Nook and offer her own inventory for sale.

Once the call was done, I noticed Jillian on her feet. She took my hand and pulled me along behind her. Up the stairs we went, with the corgis in hot pursuit.

"Where are we going?" I inquired.

My wife emerged from her library's secret door and angled left. The indoor pool, at nearly twenty feet wide by over fifty long, lay before us. We skirted around the water's edge and passed the gym that was on our right. The garage stretched out in front of us. Four bays held room to house eight cars, but there were only three inside: Jillian's SUV, my Jeep, and housed on the far left was my 1930 Ruxton sedan.

Jillian approached a large gray panel and held her thumb against an indentation. A red light that was gently moving from right to left, which I insist looks like the roving eye of a Cylon from *Battlestar Galactica*, winked out and switched colors to green. We heard a loud click and the panel swung open.

The keys to practically every gizmo we had hung on pegs inside. Jillian claimed her set and ushered us to her car. Typically, I drive for her, but not this time. I loaded the dogs in the back and I was able to slide into the passenger seat before she hit the gas.

"What's the rush? Where are we going?"

"Cookbook Nook. I need to start making some plans."

"The signing won't be for a few weeks. We have time,

you know."

"We are *not* going to procrastinate about this, Zachary. I need to see what we'll have to do in order to make the store ready to handle that many people."

"You've hosted events before," I argued. "This one shouldn't be any different, right?"

"You're a very talented writer," Jillian began, as she guided the car along our driveway. She executed a right turn and began the short trip into town. "Everyone loves that Ireland book. And, you've written a sequel. I wouldn't be surprised if every resident in PV stops by for a signed copy, and that doesn't include Medford and the surrounding areas. No, we need to figure this out."

Once we had arrived at Jillian's store, and she had wandered off to begin making notes on what needed to happen, I was approached by several teenagers. Leading the way was one very familiar red-headed girl. This one worked in the store and just so happened to be the manager. But, Sydney was wearing normal clothes, consisting of a blue and white striped blouse, jeans, and sneakers, so this suggested it was her day off.

Sydney saw me looking at her and she immediately turned to her friends and said something in a hushed tone. Her three companions hung back and watched as I neared. As for the dogs, well, they had already spotted someone they knew, and somehow I knew that if I were to let them go, they'd race each other to see who could get to her first.

"Hi, Sydney. Why so pensive? Looks like you guys are working up the courage to ask me something, and your support group appears to have just stiffed you with the bill."

Sydney stifled a giggle. "I'm sorry. You're right. I was

going to approach Mrs. Anderson about this, but she seems preoccupied."

"You're not working today, are you?" I asked.

"No, it's my day off. I was rehears--, uh, that is …"

"Out with it, kiddo. What can I do for you?"

Sydney's mouth opened, only nothing came out. She angrily shook her head and took a deep breath. "Okay, here it is. My friends and I were … oh, I'm sorry. I really should make the introductions first. Guys? Come here. This is Mr. Anderson. He's the famous writer I was telling you about, and down there—that's Sherlock and Watson."

Three kids slowly approached. One was an African-American boy of sixteen, wearing a dark button-down shirt and khaki pants; the second was a blonde girl who looked as though she could be captain of the cheerleading team. Then again, that might be due to the fact that she was, in fact, wearing a cheerleader's uniform. The third kid was an Asian girl who was probably the same age as Sydney. She was dressed in an all-white outfit, including blouse and pants, and was wearing a thin yellow vest. She also had on a yellow fedora-type hat. Personally, I thought it was very stylish.

Sydney pointed at the boy.

"We have Deion Johnson, Maddy Fisher, who for some reason thought it was appropriate to wear her cheerleader uniform here, and finally, Yoona Park. Mr. Anderson, we belong to a, uh, … no, I can't do this. Yoona? Put your hand down. As I was saying, we created a drama club, where we like to rehearse our favorite Shakespearean plays."

Having no clue where this was going, I waited patiently for the girl to get to the point.

"We, uh, that is to say, *I* learned that your new house

has its own theater. Is that true?"

I thought back to my large movie room located on the ground floor. "It does. I'm not sure how this helps you."

"Well, we were wondering if we might be able to rehearse there."

That's when the cobwebs cleared and I figured out what Sydney wanted.

"The theater with the stage," I said. "Sorry, and I can't believe I have to say this, but with regards to *that* house, you have to be more specific. The movie theater is on the bottom floor, and the *theatre*," using my phony British accent for the word, and thereby earning myself a giggle, "is located on the next floor up, above the pool."

"You have an indoor pool?" Yoona asked. "How lucky are you?"

"I do, and incredibly so," I said, grinning at the girl. "So, you guys are asking for permission to rehearse at my house, in the theatre with the stage, is that it?"

Sydney nodded hopefully. Jillian wandered by at that moment and hesitated when she saw her manager.

"Sydney? Aren't you supposed to have the day off?"

"I'm here to pick up another set of bamboo spoons," the girl clarified. "Yoona burnt my last set."

"It's not my fault your stove heats up so fast."

"It's a gas stove," Sydney said, rolling her eyes. "Open flames? Wood spoon? Hello! Of course, it's going to catch fire."

"I was about to give these kids permission to use the theatre and the stage," I told my wife. "They formed a Shakespeare club, and were looking for a place to perform."

Jillian nodded. "As long as you don't mind an audience, feel free. Put together a schedule and let us know."

Sydney clapped excitedly and leapt forward to embrace the two of us in a three-way hug. Once the kids were gone, Jillian looked at me and shook her head.

"I can't leave you alone for a second, can I?"

I gave her a *what can you do* grin and headed for the lounge, a small reading area near the center of the store.

"Who would've thought this week would be so exciting?" I asked the dogs. Sherlock snorted once and jumped up onto my lap. He settled into the space between my right leg and the chair and I swear the little booger *pushed*. "We're going to have a great time this weekend, guys. You'll see."

Well, I wasn't wrong. Stories would be told for years to come. Some would focus on the events at the convention. Most, though, would involve what would happen at *Corgi Cottage*.

TWO

Okay, yes, I'm a fan of many movies," I was saying, as I held the door open for Jillian to enter. The dogs and I followed closely behind. "After all, my movie library numbers in the thousands. I can even say that there are quite a few of them I can quote from memory. However, at no time *ever* would I show up at one of these things wearing something like *that*."

I was referring to the large group of people we had just passed who were dressed as their favorite characters from at least five different fantasy movies. I saw the swirling black coat belonging to one ranger and would-be king, the brown and green tunic that his elven best friend often wore, and sure enough, trailing along after them was either a small kid or an actual dwarf playing, well, a dwarf.

"What's the matter, Zachary?" my wife teased. "You don't like dressing up?"

"I really don't," I confessed. "It's bad enough when I have to dress up in a tuxedo, but to walk around in a getup like that? No, thanks. I don't care how good the movie might be."

As you have probably figured out, it was now Friday, and the Southern Oregon Comic Con had officially started. Proudly wearing our VIP badges around our necks, Jillian and I stepped inside and came to an abrupt stop. I don't know what I was thinking I'd find in here, but this certainly wasn't it.

Firstly, I was assuming we'd be going to Medford for this convention, but no. We were in Central Point, which shares its southern border with Medford. Why were we here? Well, it was the home of the Jackson County fairgrounds and a very large convention center. I found out later that the event's location was changed at the last minute. Apparently, someone had badly misjudged the number of tickets that would be sold. Granted, it didn't sell out, but oh, did they come close!

The interior of the convention had been decorated with huge swaths of black fabric and hundreds, if not thousands, of tiny LED lights, giving visitors the feeling that they were walking through outer space. Vendor tables were everywhere, ranging in size from ten-by-ten booths to ten-by-forty. Bobbleheads, build-your-own knock-off laser swords, collectors displaying huge Lego creations, and a booth dedicated to selling old-school VHS movie tapes were the first booths we saw, and those were only the tables facing the front entrance. Many, many additional rows were behind, extending several hundred feet back.

I must've seen a dozen Princess Leias, several girls dressed as Wednesday Addams, and an ingenious fellow who had welded a pair of wagon wheels to his trash can and painted it to look like R2-D2. I will also say there were an absolute ton of people dressed as their favorite anime characters, but since I know absolutely nothing about them, I'll leave it at that. And mascots! We saw someone dressed as a life-sized peanut, someone I'm hoping was the Jolly Green Giant, and we even saw a rotund older fellow walking around with a monocle in his eye, wearing a tuxedo and a top hat.

Sherlock and Watson were beyond excited. To be in a room with hundreds of people had to be their ultimate fantasy. Spider-Man, Wonder Woman, and even Superman stopped to give each of the dogs a pat on the head. One Stormtrooper recognized the corgis and called out their names as he walked by.

I felt a tap on my shoulder. Jillian was pointing at an area directly ahead of us that had rows of folding chairs set out in a semi-circle around a podium and a screen. Most of the chairs were filled, and some type of presentation was already underway. Upon a closer look, I could see it was a trailer for some CGI movie, only I didn't recognize it. That's when I heard the narrator say something about the official trailer dropping in a few hours, and that the movie studio was dumping millions of dollars into the advertising budget.

We spotted some empty seats near the back, and settled down to watch what was being touted as next summer's biggest blockbuster. Maybe I'm getting old? Perhaps my patience wasn't what it used to be? Whatever the reason, I found myself rolling my eyes at the antics on the screen. Yes, the CGI animals were amazingly realistic, but no, I didn't think I'd like watching a movie with a leading man who was a turtle walking upright, on his two legs. Just because a movie *could* do something, doesn't mean they *should*.

"Seems rather silly, don't you think?" Jillian whispered in my ear.

"Roger that. I think I'll pass. I don't recognize any of the voices, the story looks depressing, and the humor seems … forced. Uh, oh. Did you want to see it?"

Jillian shook her head. "I will pass, too."

The presentation finished, and the audience politely clapped its approval. The narrator smoothly switched gears and announced the next trailer. The screen darkened and the cockpit of a starfighter was shown, with stars streaking by as it sped through space. The small fighter banked sharply as it aggressively struggled to lose its pursuer. A bolt of light appeared and vaporized the craft several seconds later.

A triumphant fanfare of music blasted through the speakers, startling the entire audience. The dogs fired off a few warning woofs, as if to say they didn't appreciate being spooked, either. The music … sounded familiar. It wasn't until I closed my eyes and listened to the theme play that the answer came to me. Sighing, I opened my eyes and scowled.

"What is it?" Jillian asked. "Do you know which movie this is?"

"It's a remake," I sighed. "Another one. *The Last Starfighter*. When will they leave well enough alone? There's nothing wrong with the first one."

"*The Last Starfighter*," Jillian repeated, nodding. "I recognize the music now, too. You're right. Why would they want to remake that movie?"

"Because Hollywood is clearly running out of original ideas. Why come up with something new when you can take an original and make it worse?"

"We should really wait to see it before passing judgement," Jillian told me. "You never know. It might be good. Remember what you said about the *Jumanji* remake."

"Yeah, yeah. Are you going to keep bringing that up every time I mention *remake*?"

My wife grinned and didn't say anything.

The screen brightened and showed a run-down trailer park. Well, so far, so good. Then, a girl in her late teens, playing an arcade game. A crowd of onlookers, both young and old, cheered her on. With a start, I realized what they did.

Hollywood, in its supreme brilliance, had decided to play the let's-remake-this-movie-using-a-female-lead card. Now, I don't have a problem with movies featuring an all-women cast. My only requirement was to keep the story original. Leave the remakes out of it. To prove my point, all I had to do was bring up a certain ghost-catching fiasco from a few years ago. To say it was poorly received was an understatement. I would rather use *Ocean's 8* as an example. An all-female cast, in their own separate story, had a much better chance of getting me to purchase a ticket.

I heard a collective groan from the audience. I'm guessing I wasn't the only one tired of remakes. The narrator, sensing this, immediately launched into a question and answer session from the audience.

"Yep, they lost me," I told Jillian.

"Me, too, I'm afraid. Want to head over there? I think I see someone I'd like you to meet."

"Oh? Alright, let's go. I've got the leashes."

"I think they ought to make one of your books into a movie," Jillian said, as we slowly made our way past row after row of vendor tables and booths. "Has anyone ever approached you about it?"

"Honestly? No. But, it isn't the first time I've heard it. I get fan emails every month that suggests one of my books should be made into a movie, or at the very least, a television movie."

"I think the Ireland book is a strong contender."

I shrugged. "*Heart of Éire* is definitely the most popular book I've ever written. However, it'd have to be turned into a screenplay in order for that to happen, and that is something I don't have any experience doing."

We stopped at a booth selling books. I noticed a small rack of leather-bound hardcovers and headed for a closer look. A guy was standing nearby, with his back to me, reading from a book he was holding. My first clue that something was amiss should've been noticing what my wife was doing. More specifically, the fact that she wasn't selecting any books. Instead, she hung behind me for a few moments, watching.

A book title caught my attention. Written in delicate gold-leaf lettering on a dark leather-bound cover was the title and author: *The Princess Bride*, by William Goldman. I gently opened the book to inspect the pages and saw, much to my delight, that there were illustrations scattered throughout the book. With a price tag just shy of thirty dollars, I decided that a treasured story, presented in a gorgeous package such as this, belonged in our library.

"What did you find?" my wife asked, as she tried to look over my shoulder. "*The Princess Bride*? Excellent choice. I have a paperback copy, and it's nowhere near this nice."

"Have you ever read the original?" the man standing just off my right suddenly asked me.

I hadn't looked up from the book yet. "This *is* the original, in its unabridged glory."

The man approached and I finally glanced up. He held out a hand. "May I?"

"Uh, er, sure."

The stranger took the book and opened it. He grunted once and showed me the second or third page.

"There, do you see this? It says *S. Morgenstern's Classic Tale of True Love and High Adventure*. That's a quote, by the way. I've tried to find this S. Morgenstern, but haven't had any luck. What about you? Ever find the original?"

I was looking directly into the eyes of Bruce Campbell, star of the *Evil Dead* series. Well, almost. After all, he was slightly taller than me. Bruce noticed movement on my left, glanced at Jillian, and smiled at her.

I held out my hands, indicating I wanted the book. Once I was holding it, I carefully closed it and held out a hand.

"Zachary Anderson. It's a pleasure, Mr. Campbell."

Bruce shook my hand and gave me a friendly slap on my shoulder. "Always a pleasure to meet a fan. So, have you ever found the original book that one is based on? My wife is a fan, and I'd love to find the original for her."

"There isn't one," I told the actor. "Believe it or not, this was a ruse that William Goldman maintained up until the day he died. S. Morgenstern is a fictitious Florin writer. I'm an author myself, and one day a few years ago, on a whim, I did the same thing you were doing and looked it up 'cause I was thinking along the same lines. Imagine my surprise when I learned the same thing."

"Well, I'll be. Brother, you've saved me a lot of time. Thanks."

The actor wandered off. I looked at Jillian with what I'm sure was the biggest, goofiest smile ever.

"You enjoyed that," she mock-accused.

"What do you think? That was so cool! Great taste in books, too." Turning, I pulled up the lanyard holding my VIP pass. A few moments later, I took her hand and kissed it. "Best present ever!"

Delighted, my wife slipped her arm through mine and, together, we headed deeper into the throng of bustling people. We only made it a few steps when I felt the leashes go taut, as if both dogs had suddenly hit the brakes. Turning, I looked back at Sherlock, only he wasn't looking at me, but at something off to the right. Watson was sitting next to him and was also looking in the same direction.

"What are you guys doing?" I asked, giving the leashes a gentle tug. "We're going *this* way."

"Awwooowooo," Sherlock howled, choosing to keep his vocalization low and argumentative.

"What's the matter?" Jillian asked. "What are they staring at?"

At that moment, a large figure appeared in a gap between the panels that had been set up to cordon off certain areas. I might not know who was in the costume, but I had to tip my hat to them. It had to be the most elaborate outfit I had ever seen, whether in person or on the internet.

I was looking at Optimus Prime, of the Transformers.

Shiny metal glinted under the lights as the eight-foot-tall figure strode by us, making a loud clunking noise with each step. I stared at the figure as they walked, admiring how whomever was concealed within the costume would have to be walking on stilts. Not only did he have to be up on stilts to be that tall, he was pulling it off beautifully. I would have fallen flat on my face with the first step.

"Oooooooo!" Watson moaned, also using a low growl.

Both corgis were sitting, and both were watching the figure as he passed us. Was I supposed to be paying attention to the leader of the Autobots? Before he could completely pass us, I whipped out my cell and snapped a couple of pictures.

"Transformers?" Jillian asked. Her skepticism was apparent. "Why would they want us to look at the Transformers?"

I shrugged. "No idea. I took the picture and look at them now. They're both up and walking as though nothing happened. This is the part where I usually say we have ourselves our first corgi clue, only we're not working a case."

This. This right here. I figure this was the point in time when I jinxed myself and life gave me a brutal reality check. How do I know this? Because of what happens next.

Four police officers passed us less than ten seconds later, headed in the same direction we were. One of them glanced down as they passed and, seeing Sherlock and Watson, came to an immediate stop. His surprised eyes sought mine and I now know why he hesitated.

It was Officer DeVos, from the Medford police. He is one of Vance's many friends from the various police forces around us. We met him a couple of months ago, when we were investigating thefts of ice cream.

"Zack! Jillian! What are you doing here? And there's Sherlock and Watson. Are you here because of the theft, too?"

My head jerked up. "What was that? Something was stolen?"

DeVos nodded. "That's right. From what we were told, it happened less than an hour ago. I guess the security here thought they could solve the case themselves, but seeing how they don't have a suspect, they reached out to us."

"Do you know what was taken?" Jillian asked.

Officer DeVos pulled out a small flip notebook and consulted his notes. "It has a weird name. I had to write it down to make sure I didn't mess anything up. Let's see. One M41-A pulse rifle. And before you ask, no, I have no idea what that could be. Obviously, it's something important to this room full of nerds, so …"

"Officer?" Jillian interrupted. "We're here because both Zachary and I are, as you would call them, nerds."

DeVos hung his head. "I apologize, ma'am. I shouldn't have said that. Zack, your expression tells me you know what was stolen."

I shrugged. "I know I've heard it from somewhere, but …"

"Think mid-1980s," Jillian urged.

"That's not much help," I said.

"It's the weapon used to fight off an alien attack," Jillian told me.

"Still not helping," I said, sighing.

My wife smiled. "Oh, I'll bet I can bring you around. Let's try this. This particular gun was presented by Corporal Hicks to …"

"… Ripley," I finished, as the rusty wheels finally started turning. "It's the rifle Hicks used to teach Ripley how to defend herself on planet LV 426."

"And who's Hicks?" Officer DeVos wanted to know. "He's a corporal in the military? Do we know which branch? And planet *what*?"

"He's a fictitious character," I told the officer.

"Oh, roger that. The comic con. I should've seen that coming. So, this gun was from a movie? Which one?"

"*Aliens*," I answered. "Directed by James Cameron and released in 1986. Hicks is the only marine who survives by the end of the movie."

Officer DeVos stiffened with surprise. "Oh. Holy crap. I stand corrected. I *have* heard of this. A squad of marines against a planet full of aliens. I loved that movie!"

"And Michael Biehn is here somewhere," I breathed, as I realized who must've brought the gun. I looked at DeVos and stared at him. "Oh, come on. I know you know who that is. He played Hicks. He was in *Terminator*. He was fantastic as Johnny Ringo."

DeVos' face lit up. "*Tombstone*! Of course! It made me love western movies all over again! Hey, we gotta get this back to him."

"Tell me about it," I said. "This is the first convention southern Oregon has had in a few years, and this is how we start things off? On behalf of all Oregonians, I'm ashamed to say that this happened in our state. You're right. We've got to figure out who took the gun, and how we can get it back before it's sold to some private collector."

DeVos nodded. "Look, I've got to run. I've still got your number. I'll keep you posted, 'kay?"

"Thanks, pal."

Once the policeman hurried off, I made sure Sherlock and Watson's leashes were securely wrapped around my hand before following Jillian. We wove our way around elves, goblins, witches, and a few young, aspiring wizards. There were so many people moving about, dressed in all manner of costumes, that it made me uncertain how the dogs were going to handle all of this. But, once I saw them pretty much ignoring the people wandering by, I knew I was worrying for nothing. The corgis *knew*. Somehow, Sherlock and Watson knew we were now on a case. The problem was, it wasn't official. We hadn't been asked to intervene, and I'm pretty sure it was going to stay that way. However, if my supposition was true, and this special stolen space gun *did* belong to a certain celebrity I was hoping to meet, then I wanted to help. Thankfully, I could tell Jillian was on board, too.

We arrived at a number of booths that didn't have any type of memorabilia for sale at all. Tables had been set out, with stacks of pictures laid out and cups full of pens next to them. Chairs and bottles of water could be seen everywhere. The four of us passed by some familiar faces, where I knew I had seen them before in *something*. Movie, or television show, it didn't matter.

"There's Woody," Jillian said, as she squeezed my hand.

Spencer Woodson was the owner of Toy Closet, a hobby store in PV. Woody, as he preferred to be called, has a young daughter, Chloe, who often puppysat for us when we couldn't be there with Sherlock and Watson. As we made our way over to him, a young warrior princess, popular in the late nineties, arrived at Woody's side.

"Hey Zack, hi Jillian! Wait, before either of you say anything, I need to ask you to settle something for me."

I nodded. "Sure, what's up?"

Woody pointed at Chloe's costume. "Settle an argument, would you? Would you say *this* is too provocative of a costume for a thirteen-year-old to wear? Short leather dress, decorative metal chest plate, arm band, gauntlet, and knee guards?"

"Daaaaaad," the teenager complained. "She's *supposed* to look like this."

"Please. Chloe, no one knows who you're supposed to be. It just looks like you're exposing yourself for no reason."

"You look like a famous warrior princess," I told the teenager.

A huge smile appeared on the girl's face. She hurried to my side and hooked her arm through mine.

"There! See? I told you people would know it. Thank you, Mr. Anderson."

"Proof positive that I'm getting up there in years," I chuckled. "Sorry, Woody. She's not wrong. A lot of people will recognize her in that getup. And look! She's got the trademark hula hoop of death strapped to her side."

"It's a *chakram*," Chloe clarified, as she held up the flat metal loop strapped to her waist, "and before you ask, no, I haven't tried throwing it. Yet."

"Make sure you get that battle cry of hers down," I laughed.

Chloe smiled. "Absolutely!"

"I think you look great, Chloe," Jillian told her.

"Thank you, Mrs. Anderson."

"You two are certainly not helping my case," Woody complained.

We could still hear the father and daughter arguing as

we headed off. As we moved further into the convention, it amazed me to see just how many different things were for sale. People were selling fan art, custom knives, and even knitted dolls wielding all manner of weapons.

I noticed more booths selling books and was about to head over there when nature caught up to me and I realized that downing my large soda before arriving here was clearly a very bad move to make.

"What is it?" Jillian asked, when she saw me hesitate and scan the immediate surroundings.

"I do believe I need to find a restroom."

"Oh." My wife joined me in the search. "I don't really see any signs for them, but you know they must have some here."

"I'm hoping they aren't those outdoor toilets that construction crews use."

"Looking for the restroom?" a friendly female voice asked.

"I am," I said, as I turned to the newcomer. The owner of the voice was probably in her early forties, had long curly blonde hair, and a face I *know* I've seen before. "Is it close?"

The woman pointed toward a wall.

"Go through the gap there. Once you hit that hallway, turn left. It'll be on your left-hand side. That one doesn't have any signs, so it's fairly private. If you see my husband, ask him what's taking him so long, would you?"

"Yeah, sure. Thanks. My dear? I'll be right back."

Following the directions I had been given, I found the restroom fairly easily. A man about the same height as me, dressed in black, was there. He was facing away from me, hunched over, washing his hands in the sink. Once my business was done, and the self-flushing urinal rinsed itself, I approached the next sink over and commenced washing my own hands. Finished, the stranger moved to inspect the options for drying. In his case, he elected to use paper towels instead of the automatic hand-dryer-blower-thingamajig.

I've never cared for silence when encountering another person, especially in a restroom. I usually try to come up with something to help break the ice. Nine times out of ten, a little bit of humor does the trick.

"Never should have had the soda before coming here," I said, as I finished washing my hands and moved to the paper towel dispenser.

The man in black nodded. Even though he wasn't facing me, I could see his hair was brown, his physique was on the leaner side, and I could see a few wrinkles on his face, although, who was I to judge? I had my own fair share of reminders that I wasn't a spring chicken anymore. The man nodded.

"Yep, that'll do it to you."

His voice was oddly familiar.

"Did you hear about the theft?" I asked. "The cops are here, presumably looking for this stolen movie prop."

"I heard that, too," the man admitted. "I don't suppose you know who took it, do you?"

"I'm sorry, I don't," I said. "The only thing I know is that it was used in a really famous movie; I just hope they can find it. The last thing I want to see happen is for that gun to find its way onto some collector's mantel. This theft makes us look bad, that's for sure."

"I couldn't agree more," the man agreed.

He then exited the restroom, with me following behind

him. We both appeared to be headed in the same direction, which was awkward, to say the least. Our business was done, and I was fully expecting the two of us to go our separate ways, but much to my surprise, we both headed back the way I had come. In fact, I could still see Jillian talking with the blonde woman from before. This time, though, a young boy of around seven or eight was with her. Before I could say anything, Jillian hurried over. Or, I should say the dogs quickly pulled her over. They had spotted the stranger and wanted to say hello.

"Sherlock? Watson? Stop what you're doing before you pull Jillian off her feet. Not everyone you see is a dog lover."

"It's okay," the man assured me. "I like dogs. I have one back home, too."

A few things happened here, all at the same time. I heard Jillian gasp, both corgis came to a stop just before they could jump up on my new buddy, and finally, I got a clear look at his face.

It was Michael Biehn.

The iconic sci-fi actor was staring down at my two dogs with a smile on his face. Now that I got a good look at him, I had to admit he was taller than I thought. He was easily the same height as me, making him six feet tall. Of all the movies I've seen him in, for some reason, I thought he was shorter. His physique was lean, his eyes were piercing, making someone want to think twice before approaching, but the smile he was wearing made you forget about any misgivings you might have. He held out a hand.

"Michael Biehn."

I could only shake my head and reflect on the silliness of this situation. Good God, I had just peed next to

Corporal Hicks!

"Zack Anderson. This is my wife, Jillian. Down there are Sherlock and Watson."

"Cute dogs. Love their names."

"Sorry for the comment about the stolen gun," I said. "I can only assume it was yours."

Michael sighed. "My wife told me it would be a bad idea to bring that thing here and, I'm sorry to say I didn't listen to her. My publicist is the one who suggested I do this. Oh, hey, Jen, I didn't see you standing there. Come here, would you?"

The blonde woman who had been talking with Jillian appeared by Michael's side and took his hand in hers. She flashed a smile at me before reaching for the young boy's hand. That's where I've seen her! This is Jennifer Blanc-Biehn, Michael's wife. She is also an actor, having performed in a number of movies and television shows. I seem to recall hearing they had a young son together. This must be him!

The boy noticed Sherlock and Watson and immediately pulled his hand free from his mother's. Child and corgis stared at one another. I stifled a chuckle. Let the stare-down begin. It might have started as a staring contest, but quickly progressed to a full-body wriggling battle. I actually think Sherlock was winning this round.

"I'm sorry this happened," the woman was saying. "We'll get it back, love. We have to trust the police to … oh, I'm sorry, who's this?"

Michael gently steered his wife over to us. "Jen, this is Zack and …"

"Jillian," Jennifer interrupted. "We met just a bit ago. She was telling me all about what wonderful dogs they have. Aren't they cute?"

Michael nodded. "Very. You two live around here, is that right?"

"We do," I confirmed. "Pomme Valley."

Jennifer draped her arm around the boy's shoulders. "And this is Dashiel, our son. Say hi, Dash."

"Hello," the boy offered. He only had eyes for the corgis. "Can I pet them?"

Sherlock and Watson were all but writhing with excitement. Knowing the corgis wanted to give the boy a full initiation into the pack, I looked for a suitable place for the kid to get the corgi-love he was about to receive.

"What's the matter?" Michael asked. He noticed me looking about and became concerned. "Do those two not like people?"

"The dogs want to meet him," I assured him, using a low voice. "However, both dogs can get a little … energetic, so I'm looking for the best place for your son to get knocked on his butt."

Michael chuckled, whispered a few words into Jennifer's ear, and then simply pointed down.

"Right here will do. Son, do me a favor and sit down."

The boy blinked at his father with uncomprehending eyes. "Huh? Why?"

"Trust me. You want to meet the dogs? Sit down. There you go."

I held up a hand, signaling the dogs to wait. Once I got the parents' permission, I released both dogs.

Sherlock and Watson raced each other to see who could make it to Dash first. Sherlock won. My tri-color corgi leapt onto Dashiel's chest and started giving him doggie kisses. Watson joined him a split second later. Together, with their combined weight, poor Dashiel was forced onto his back. That's when both dogs promptly sat on the boy's chest and gave him well-timed doggie kisses.

"Ackbpth! They're strong!"

Jennifer had pulled out her phone and was filming. Dashiel giggled with delight as he tried to avoid the corgis' long tongues.

"Okay, that's long enough," I decided. "Sherlock? Watson? Let him up, guys."

Jennifer suddenly put her phone away and looked at us in a new light.

"What?" I asked.

"Their names—Sherlock and Watson? Of course! You guys were in England not that long ago, weren't you? That's where I've seen you. You were on TV, meeting the Queen of England!"

Jillian nodded. "That's right. We were married in Westminster Abbey."

"The detective dogs," Jennifer breathed. She looked at Michael and gave him a victorious smile. "That's perfect! They can help us find your missing gun!"

THREE

Saturday morning started just like any other weekend. Jillian left early, telling me she had a full day scheduled at her store. It was time for the monthly inventory check. I knew from experience that it takes Jillian the entire day to go through everything, and I do mean *everything*, on her shelves and compare it to what *should* be there. It was a task that was best performed by people who were intimately familiar with the layout of the store, knew where certain items could be found, and how the point-of-sale software operated.

That essentially ruled me out.

I have helped on a few occasions, but I do believe Jillian was only humoring me after I volunteered to help.

She knew, as well as I did, I would only be getting in the way, so she was perfectly fine with giving me her blessing to return to the convention, especially after agreeing to help a famous actor retrieve a movie prop. However, since I wanted to refresh my memory about this M41-A pulse rifle, and I wanted to stall for time so that my wife could finish her store's inventory that much sooner, the dogs and I sat down to watch *Aliens* in our theater downstairs.

I ended up pausing the movie during the part in which Cpl. Hicks explained to Ripley how the Marines' favored pulse rifle worked. Sherlock and Watson barely moved as I stepped in front of the huge fireplace and gazed up at the screen. Figuring I'd never get a better shot than this, and that I could use a reference image in case I needed it later, I snapped a picture.

Sherlock and Watson, reclining on the couch and only barely keeping an eye on me, suddenly perked up. Sherlock stared at me, as though he disapproved of me taking a picture without his permission. I pointed at the screen.

"That gun, right there. See it? That's what was stolen. Someone walked out of the convention yesterday with that thing in their possession. *That* is what we need to find. We're not going to search for this based on an official request. Quite the contrary, we're doing this for the owner of that gun. He's a famous movie star, guys. Him right there. He's the one holding it. If ever there was a time to impress me, now's the time to do it, 'kay?"

Sherlock lowered his head, until it was resting on his front paws, and promptly closed his eyes. Watson had never bothered to see what I was doing in the first place, so she promptly closed her eyes and went out, like a light. Sighing, I turned back to the screen and unfroze the movie.

Wouldn't it be something if I could somehow reunite that gun with its owner? Would that mean a celebrity would owe me a favor? Wouldn't that be cool?

Once the movie had finished, and the credits began to roll, I roused the dogs and slowly stood. The three of us then went through a brief stretching process, where the dogs both unkinked their backs, and I slowly walked around the couch. The dogs quickly resumed their position on the couch. Both of my legs had fallen asleep, though, so I kept going. When you had two dense bricks snuggled up on either side of you, looking so freakin' cute you didn't want to disturb then, well, it served you right. A sense of puppy paralysis was inevitable.

"I think I'm getting too old for this," I lamented, as I leaned over the couch to check on the dogs. Both had moved to claim the recently vacated warm spot on the couch and were giving me a look which said I'd have to physically pick up their dead carcasses and move them myself before they'd have any intention of changing position on their own. "Come on, guys. Let's go for a ride, shall we?"

Sherlock was barking even before he hit the ground. He zipped by me and bolted up the stairs, with Watson hot on his heels.

"Yep. Don't mind me. I'll make it up there sooner or later."

Ruxton or Jeep? Showoff or practical? I opted for the attention-getting, head-turning Ruxton and loaded my dogs. It may get tiring having to turn down so many purchase offers—or trades—when I was in my classic roadster, but it's an absolute joy to drive.

Once we entered Jillian's store, the first person I saw

was Cookbook Nook's manager, Sydney, sitting cross-legged on the floor while she slowly went through a large pile of cookbooks.

"Three on pastry flowers," Sydney called, in a loud voice.

"I see them," Jillian's voice filtered down, from above. My wife had probably set up her laptop on one of the café's tables. "What's next?"

"Uh, let's just call them some very specific cake decorating books. Honestly, I didn't know we had these for sale."

"Wait. I know the ones you're talking about. What are they doing down there? Holy cow. Does one of them show a girl on a boat? Wearing ..."

"... very little," Sydney continued, after Jillian trailed off. "Yes. There are only two. Looks like a part one and a part two."

"Pull those. They belong in my office. I have no idea how they ended up on the floor."

"Mr. Anderson is here."

"Is he? Zachary, did you bring the dogs?"

"We're all here," I called. "You've got me curious. What books are you talking about?"

My wife descended the stairs. "Do you remember those specialty fantasy decorating books I ordered a while back? It teaches you how to create castles, dragons, and fantasy creatures?"

"I do."

"I didn't realize they were part of a larger set. To be honest, I had forgotten about them, but I did want the set, just in case someone would ask for them. Little did I know someone was talented enough to come up with some very risqué designs. Impressive, but inappropriate. I can only imagine someone found them in the back room and decided to put them on the shelf."

"When you say risqué, just how …?"

"Adult eyes only," Jillian confirmed. She looked at me and waggled a finger. "Don't get any ideas for your next birthday cake."

I pulled out my wallet and held up a credit card. "Sydney? You wanna ring me up?"

"You goof," Jillian laughed, swatting my hand away. "Don't you dare. Sydney, stay where you are. Now, I know you're not here to help me with my inventory check. Is there something you needed?"

"It's getting close to lunch. Thought I could tempt you with lunch at Casa de Joe's?"

"Oh, so very tempting. However, if I don't get this done today, then I'll have to start all over tomorrow. I'd rather not do that. You go ahead."

"And eat by myself? How boring is that?"

"I'm sure I could be tempted to go," a new voice piped up.

Vance appeared and joined us at the checkout counter.

"Hey there, stranger!" Jillian said, as she straightened a few items on the countertop. "What brings you to my establishment today?"

"I needed to talk to *him*," Vance said. "Hi Sherlock. Watson. Hang on, I've got something for you guys."

Two corgi rumps hit the ground in record time.

"I'd be surprised if you didn't," I said, as the dogs crunched through their treats. "What's on your mind, pal?"

"Well, your nerd theft, it …"

"My *nerd theft*?" I repeated, chuckling. "You're referring

to the theft of one M41-A pulse rifle?"

Vance checked his notes. "Yeah. That's exactly right. Wow. Does everyone know what this thing is besides me?"

"I *did* just watch *Aliens* a couple of hours ago," I admitted. "I wanted a closer look at that rifle."

"Cheater," Vance accused.

"Why don't you two go to lunch?" Jillian suggested. "And wherever you end up, would you pick me up something?"

I gave my wife a kiss. "Always. I'll find something."

"Thank you, Zachary."

Jillian returned to the second floor and disappeared from sight. Moments later, I could hear Sydney resume her vocal checks with my wife as they sorted through their stock.

"I never turn down free lunch," Vance said, as he gleefully rubbed his hands together. "Where are we going?"

I pointed at the dogs. "We'll be headed to …"

Vance looked up when I didn't finish my sentence, then turned to see where I was looking. A guy dressed entirely in dark colors, including jeans, sneakers, shirt, and sweatshirt, walked through the door. His shirt had large white lettering on it, advertising something about a history website. He was also wearing dark sunglasses and a black baseball cap, with a website displayed in bright white letters:

www.SettingHistoryStraight.com

At the same time the man took off his sunglasses, I heard a jingling coming from one of the dogs, so I dropped my gaze to the floor. For the record, I'd like it known that I still hadn't looked at his face. I was too busy committing the advertised website to memory, so that I could take a look later.

"What is it?" Vance wanted to know. "Did they pick something up?"

I shrugged. "Not that I can tell."

"Omigod," a girl's voice suddenly said.

I snapped my head up. That was Sydney. Had something happened?

Cookbook Nook's manager was on her feet and staring at us. Hmm, let's go with *looking through us*. It looked like the poor girl had just seen a ghost, and based on the way she was behaving, it was currently behind us.

Vance and I turned at the same time. There, grinning at me like the Cheshire Cat from *Alice in Wonderland*, was Michael Biehn. Vance looked at me with shock written all over his features. Ignoring him, I waved Michael over.

"Hey there. Tell me this isn't a coincidence."

"The mother of all," Michael said, as he shook my hand. He turned to Vance and nudged me on my shoulder. "Friend of yours?"

"Oh, sorry. Introductions. Michael, this is my good friend, Vance. Over there, with her mouth hanging open, is Sydney, manager of …"

Sydney appeared at my side in a flash, and giggling like a schoolgirl, shyly held out her hand.

"… the store here."

"I'm so thrilled to meet you," the teenager gushed. "I loved *The Abyss*. And *Aliens*? Best sequel ever!"

"I'm surprised you've seen them," Michael admitted. He shook the girl's hand and offered her a lopsided smile. "I have to say, most people your age don't recognize me."

"I love the eighties," Sydney proudly declared. "I'm

hoping to become an actress someday."

"And I'm sure you'll do great," Michael said, offering the girl a smile.

Sydney's face flushed red and she hurried away. I then turned to Vance and nodded in Michael's direction.

"Vance, I'd like you to meet Michael Biehn."

Vance thrust his hand out. "You're the one who …"

"… lost a gun?" Michael finished. "Guilty. Imagine my surprise when, as I was driving by, I see a guy with two corgis walking into a store. I said to myself, it can't be who I'm thinking it is, so I had to pull over and see."

"Where's your wife and son?" I asked.

"Jennifer and Dashiel are back at the hotel, with her mother. She frequently comes with us when we do these trips. You know, I'm surprised you're not at the convention. I noticed you had VIP passes yesterday."

"My wife asked me that this morning. Truthfully? I enjoy going with her, and I know she's busy this morning. So, I can wait until she's done. What about you? Shouldn't you be there, too?"

"I'm not due to be there until later this afternoon. I haven't been in this part of the state that much, so I wanted to look around. I'm glad I did. I like it here."

I looked at Vance, who was surprisingly silent. "Gonna say anything else?"

"I loved you in *Tombstone*."

Michael nodded as a thoughtful expression appeared on his face. "Probably the best film I've ever had a part in. Some of my best work."

A thought occurred. "Michael? Vance and I were about to head out for a bite to eat. Casa de Joe's is not that far from here. Great Mexican food. Would you like to join us?"

Michael looked down at Sherlock and Watson, who were staring at the newcomer with the hopes that he'd be armed with an endless bag of doggie treats, too.

"What about them? You can't take them with us, can you?"

"Many of the restaurants have terraces outside, and as long as the dogs stay out of the restaurant's interior, they're allowed to join us."

Michael nodded. "I like that. I wish we had places like that back home. You don't mind me tagging along?"

I shook my head. "Not at all. Want to ride with me? You can leave your car there. My wife owns this building, so it's in no danger of being towed."

"Sure. Let me get a few things first."

"No problem."

While my new celebrity friend rummaged through his rented vehicle, Vance grabbed my arm and pulled me aside.

"Zack, what the hell? Is this seriously happening?"

"Didn't I tell you? The dogs and I will be looking for this gun on behalf of the Biehn family."

My friend punched me on the arm. "No, you most certainly did not! Holy cow! I'm going to lunch with Michael Biehn. I … I really don't know what to say about that."

I lowered my voice. "Well, there are two ways to approach this. You can either choose to be freaked out by it, or you'll see that he's just a regular guy. Once he gets to know you, he'll treat you like his best friend."

"How are you handling all of this?"

I scoffed. "Me? Please. I'm still on option one. I haven't progressed to option two yet."

Vance laughed. "Okay. All right, I can do this. Wow."

"Riding with us?" Michael asked Vance, as I unlocked my car.

A goofy look appeared on my detective friend's face.

"Uh, sure. Why not? Sherlock, scooch over, would you?"

Thirty minutes later, we were seated outside, at one of the five round tables on Casa de Joe's terrace. We placed our orders and, as we started working our way through our bowl of chips, Vance cleared his throat.

"Look, Mr. Biehn, I've gotta ask you something."

"Fire away. And call me Michael."

"Michael. You got it. Okay, I wanted to know something. What was it like, working on *Tombstone*?"

The veteran actor fell silent for a moment as he considered his answer. "What do you know about the events that happened at Tombstone? The city, not the movie."

Vance shrugged. "Just what I've seen in the movies, I guess. Why do you ask?"

"Take Wyatt Earp," Michael began. "Everyone seems to think he's the epitome of a true American hero. But, would it surprise you to learn he was nothing more than a murderer and a cattle wrangler?"

At a loss for words, Vance looked at me. I gave him a shrug.

"I didn't know that. Are you sure?"

"Hollywood only got a few things right with the movie. Don't get me wrong, I was thrilled to be working alongside such a talented cast, but the Cowboys … you know, the hired guns from the movie who were wearing red-sashes? They were portrayed as being the bad guys."

"And they're not?" Vance asked.

"No. They were just hired hands. Hollywood has a habit of ignoring facts and sensationalizing the smallest, trivial bits of information. The Cowboys liked to wear those sashes, yes, so that made it in the movie. But the shootout …yes, the shootout happened, only no, the Cowboys weren't responsible. Wyatt Earp actually fired first, and what was the result? He faced murder charges. I'll bet you didn't know that, did you?"

"I didn't," Vance admitted. "If you don't mind me asking, sir, er, Michael, what made you check into the legitimacy of the story? Because you were in it?"

"I've always been fascinated with Tombstone and its role in American history. It annoys me to no end that people have so many misconceptions about what is true, and what is not. Oh, hey, see this?"

Michael opened his jacket and indicated his shirt. On it was an advertisement for the same website listed on his hat. *Setting History Straight* was written in white block letters on his dark shirt.

"I've actually written a number of articles about various topics, and was looking for a way to get them online," Michael explained. "A techie, I am *not*. Everyone I asked didn't have any idea how to start a website and get my stories online. Then, I reached out to a friend of mine and asked if he knew anything about it, and just like that, he created a website and uploaded everything I threw at him. I promote it and he handles the tech side of things. In case you haven't figured it out, I'm not the best when it comes to modern day electronics."

Vance raised a hand. "That makes two of us."

Michael tapped my arm and pointed at the street. "Love your car, brother."

I looked at my roadster and grinned. "Thanks. Everyone wants to buy it off me, but I always have to pass. My wife gave me that car after she learned it came with a house she purchased. It's a Ruxton, once owned by Dame Hilda Highland."

"Your wife gave you that car? I think I need to tell Jennifer to get with the program," Michael joked.

I slid my phone across the table. "I double dog dare you to tell it to her right now."

Laughing, Michael slid my phone back to me. "I may be getting old, but I'm no fool. Zack, Vance, I have to say that I really enjoy your town. I wasn't sure what to think when my agent suggested I accept Medford's offer to attend their convention, but I'm glad I did."

"Even though your gun was stolen?" Vance asked.

"Well, I'd be lying if I said it didn't bother me. Hell, brother, we're just going to have to let the cops do their jobs."

I pointed at Vance. "He *is* a cop. Detective, actually."

Michael gazed at Vance. "Is that so? That's a commendable occupation. Are you working this case, too?"

Vance pointed at me. "Only if he asks for help. The theft happened in Medford, which means it's out of my jurisdiction. However, I know Zack is helping you out by searching for this thing. If he needs any help, then I'm only a phone call away."

Michael fixed me with an intense stare, which I will admit, caused me to fidget in my chair. "Has any progress been made?"

I held up my hands. "Medford hasn't shared anything with me yet. I have a feeling we're on our own."

Michael nodded. "Where do we go from here?"

The longer I was with this celebrity, and the more he talked, the easier it was to believe I was just talking to a normal person. I'd like to say that I was getting over being star struck in his presence, but I wasn't. The absurdity that I was sitting in my hometown enjoying lunch with a movie star who had been in a number of my favorite movies was still mind boggling. But, when he specifically used *we* in a sentence, I had to order myself not to choke on my soda.

"What time did you say you have to be back at the convention?" I asked.

Michael checked his watch. "Not for another four hours. Do you mind if I tag along? I've never been part of an active investigation before."

Vance looked at me and gave me the *it's your call* look.

"Hey, why not? The more the merrier, right?"

The waitress came with our order. My mind spun as I dug into my carne asada burrito. It was one thing to meet a celebrity you admire, but quite another to spend an extended amount of time with them. It was all I could do to keep the smile from spreading from ear to ear.

We finished our lunch and I took care of the check. Michael clapped me on the back and slid his chair closer.

"So, what should we do now?"

I looked at Vance. "You're the official detective here, so feel free to jump in if I get something wrong, okay?"

Vance nodded. "You got it, pal."

I looked at Michael. "The gun that was stolen? It …"

"Pulse rifle," Michael corrected.

"And you call yourself a fan of *Aliens*," Vance teased. "We should go get that girl."

"Who, Sydney? Bite me. Now, as I was saying, this pulse rifle? Am I right to assume it's worth a lot of money?"

Michael slowly nodded. "To the right person, probably."

I looked at Vance. "How would someone go about selling something like that? I mean, this thing was just stolen yesterday. In order to pull something like that off, our perp our perp must be smart. So, will he try to offload the thing as soon as he can, or do you think they'd stash it and wait for all the inevitable media attention to blow over?"

Vance mulled it over for a few moments. "The second option. I'd sit on it for a couple of weeks."

I nodded. "That's what I'm thinking, too. Besides, look at the dogs. They've already given us a corgi clue."

"A corgi clue?" Michael repeated. He frowned. "I don't know what that means."

I pointed at Sherlock and Watson, who were currently napping.

"We've learned long ago that, should the dogs fixate on something, especially while we're working a case, we need to pay attention. I'll take a picture, and presto, one corgi clue. Now, those clues won't make any sense at the time, but they will later."

"Isn't that something?" Michael said, as he gazed down at the two sleeping corgis. "I wonder how they do it."

"I've been trying to figure that out for a while," I said.

"And?" Michael prompted.

In unison, Vance and I both held up our hands in a *who knows* gesture. The movie star laughed.

"I'm really starting to enjoy this. Very well. You asked about the value of the prop I used in the film. To a collector, I wouldn't be surprised if it brought in around two hundred thousand. Maybe more. Everyone seems to love that movie."

"That's certainly motive," I decided. "Vance, is there any way I could get you to use your detective powers and see if there are any other high-profile thefts that happened at comic cons? It might give us some insight."

Vance nodded and pulled out his phone. I watched him swing his legs over the waist-high fence and wander off. I felt a tap on my arm.

"Zack, let me ask you something," Michael began. "Be honest with me. Your dogs—have they really solved a number of crimes, like you've said?"

"Oh, absolutely."

Michael stared at me, and I could see the skepticism behind those piercing eyes of his. "Can you give me a few examples?"

I sat back in my chair. "Well, let's see. They've found missing items, located people who didn't want to be found, solved a cold case from over a hundred years ago, which earned them a trip to meet the Queen of England, not to mention …"

"All right, all right, I get it. I didn't mean that the way it sounded. I just find it difficult to believe two dogs can be that smart."

Both dogs woke, shook their collars, and looked up at Michael. Then, together, they sniffed the air.

"What are they doing?" Michael asked.

I stared at my dogs. "If I didn't know any better, then I'd say they were about to …"

"Woof!"

Sherlock was on his feet first. He reared up on his hind legs in an attempt to see over the small half-wall outlining the terrace we were on. When he discovered he was still too short, Sherlock let out a snort of exasperation and moved several steps away. Having never worried about either of my dogs wandering away from me, I had let the leashes drop. Now, seeing how Sherlock was about to prove me wrong, I reached for the leashes, but before I could, Sherlock turned about and raced back to Michael.

The stoic actor, who during his career, has fought off a T-800 terminator, numerous xenomorphs, and tried to out-draw Doc Holliday, gasped with surprise. A split second later, Sherlock was sitting on his lap, but ignoring him. The tri-colored corgi was interested only in what was happening on the other side of the fence and had used Michael's lap as an elevation boost.

My new friend was nodding.

"All right, I'll admit I didn't see that coming. What's he doing?"

I looked in the same direction as Sherlock. "Hmm, I'm not sure. I think he's watching the people walking by. Or maybe the cars?"

"Is this one of those corgi clues you were talking about?"

"Yeppers. Watch him for me. I'm going to start taking a few pictures. If it's a clue, then he'll lose interest as soon as the photo is taken."

Three camera clicks later, or in this case, cell phone taps, Sherlock jumped down. Michael leaned close.

"What do you see?"

I held my phone out so we could both review the pictures.

"Umm, well, here we have a family wandering by. Two parents and two kids. Then, well, the family is still visible, but the two kids have moved out of the frame. And finally, I don't know, passing traffic? Does anything in there stand out to you?"

Michael held out a hand. I passed him my phone and then watched as he slipped on a pair of glasses.

"Well, I don't think it's the family. By the third picture, all but the father is out of the frame. Or, is that the clue? Since he didn't jump down until the end, should we be looking at the father?"

"The only thing I can tell you is that it'll make sense at the end."

"Is it frustrating?" Michael asked.

"What, that *they* are smarter than me?" I let out a laugh. "A little. I don't let it get to me. At the end of a case, I get all of our friends together and we'll go through the pictures to try and figure if we're smarter than the dogs by trying to decipher what Sherlock and Watson were trying to tell us."

"Ah. I was wondering about that."

Vance returned at that moment. He saw the two of us staring at my phone and took his seat.

"Did I miss something?"

"You missed a corgi clue," I reported. "Just a few moments after you left, Sherlock woofed at something *thataway*. We have no idea what."

"Ah. You got a picture of it, is that right?"

I held up my phone. "Yep. What did you find out?"

Vance pulled out his notebook. "More than you would have thought. Jules is totally jealous, of this, by the way. Anyway, listen to this. During the last year, there have been four thefts reported at various comic cons all across the country. Prior to that, there was a rash of thefts all across Europe. First, a screen-used light sword from one of the *Star Wars* movies was taken."

"Lightsaber," both Michael and I corrected, at the same time.

Vance waved off the scorn in our voices. "Whatever."

"Which one?" I asked.

"I have no idea. All they said was that it was a light sword thingy and I moved on."

"Which movie?" Michael clarified.

"Oh. Uh, let me see. Number seven, the one with the girl and the round robot."

"What else?" I asked.

"A gold ring from …"

"… *Lord of the Rings*?" I interrupted.

Vance shook his head. "*The Hobbit*, actually. One of them. Supposedly, this one was used by the actor who played that creepy dude."

"Andy Serkis," Michael supplied.

"That's the one. Next, we have something called a *phurba*, from …"

"*The Shadow*," I answered.

"You're both nerds," Vance groaned. "Never saw it. And finally, there's something here about a key, from *The Mummy*."

I looked at Michael. It was a struggle to keep the goofy grin from my face. Here I was, having a conversation about movies, with an actual actor. Does it get any better than this?

"Key? From *The Mummy*? Does it say which one? There are a ton of them, man."

"Keys or movies?" Michael asked.

"Movies. The old one, with Bela Lugosi in it? Or maybe the one with Brendan Fraser? Or even the newer one, with Tom Cruise?"

"A key," Michael repeated, thinking hard. "I've seen the one from 1932."

"So have I," I reported.

"I don't recall a key being in it."

I nodded. "Agreed."

Michael sat back in his chair. "Then … wait, I've got it. The 1999 version, it had keys in it."

Frowning, I turned to my new friend. "It did? The one with Brendan Frasier? I've seen that movie a number of times. I don't remember anything about a key."

Michael held up his hands and cupped his fingers together. "It was about this big, and was used to open those two books, and to lock the sarcophagus holding the guy who became the mummy."

I snapped my fingers. "Got it, thanks. I had forgotten. You're talking about that metal box with the lid that springs open? I remember it now."

"I'm glad you two know what you're talking about," Vance said, shaking his head. "Whatever. You wanted to know what was taken, well, now you know."

"All are small items, easily concealed," I mused aloud. "I wonder if these thefts were committed by the same person? Or persons?"

"You're thinking more than one person pulled this off," Michael guessed.

Vance nodded. "Makes sense. It says here that every single one of these thefts was pulled off in the middle of the day. That means they were out in the open. I don't see how someone could do that unless someone *else* was creating a diversion."

"How do we proceed?" Michael asked.

"Do it again," I whispered, thinking fast.

"What was that?" Vance asked.

"We lure them out," I said. "Get them to do it again. They're going after props from well-known movies. I say we set a trap. See if we can lure them out for a repeat performance, only this time, we'll be ready."

"We'd have to coordinate with Medford police," Vance reminded us.

"I don't think that'd be a problem," Michael said. "I'm certain I could get them on board with this. But, I can't help point out the flaw in your plan, Zack. We don't have anything to use as bait. Whatever we use has to be believable, so that means the owner, like myself, should have starred in the movie the prop came from. And I'm sorry, I'm fresh out of pulse rifles."

I pulled out my phone. "I think I might have that covered. Just a sec. I need to see if I still have his number. He … there we are. Officer DeVos? Do you remember me? Yeah, that's right. Glad to hear from you, too. I … yes, as a matter of fact, I'm calling about the theft. The owner has asked me and the dogs to look into the robbery and see if we can recover his item. Yes, I know full well who owns that gun. He's sitting with me right now. Forget about that. Listen, by any chance are you anywhere near the fairgrounds? You are? Perfect. I need you to go find Bruce Campbell and hand him your phone, okay? Yes, *that* Bruce Campbell. I'll fill you in when I can. Sure, I'll wait."

"Bruce Campbell?" Vance asked, in a soft tone. "Isn't he the one who was in that movie where his hand is a chain saw?"

"*Evil Dead*," Michael said. "My wife and I are fans. What are you thinking, Zack?"

"Well, I know Bruce lives in the area. I'm thinking we

should ask him to … Bruce? Hello, this is Zack Anderson, the guy with the two corgis? I'm the one who was talking to you about *Princess Bride*? Yes, that's me. Listen, I have a huge favor to ask. By chance, did you keep any mementos from *Army of Darkness*? I'm hoping you kept a certain, uh, book. This one has … you did? You have no idea how happy I am to hear that. What's that? Why am I asking? Hoo, boy. Well, it's like this…"

I spent a total of thirty minutes explaining what we wanted to set up, and why we wanted to borrow that particular prop. In the end, it took promises from myself, from Vance, acting on behalf of the local police department, and from Michael himself before permission was given. In fact, it was the *Evil Dead* actor's idea to place his treasure into Michael's possession, suggesting the reason Michael would have it in the first place was that he was borrowing it from a friend so that the local fans wouldn't be disappointed.

I have to give credit where credit is due: movie stars are a lot smarter than most people think.

Vance took over the phone call and made arrangements to pick up the prop. Contact information was exchanged, which sent my already spinning mind reeling with shock since I now had *two* celebrity contacts on my phone, and the call was terminated. Er, no pun intended.

What a weekend. Not only was I having lunch with one celebrity, I was now willingly entering in the contact information of another. This weekend was going down in the record books, no doubt about it.

"Now what do we do?" Michael asked.

"Your wife," I began, as I turned to the actor, "she's on social media a lot?"

"Yes. She says it helps build her image, her brand. Do you need her to do something?"

"Tell her to start posting about that book," I instructed. "Make announcements that a fellow actor is loaning you a rare movie prop so that the fans will have something to see."

"In the hopes that the thieves will see it," Michael said. "That's perfect. Consider it done, Zack."

Vance looked at Michael. "What time do you have to go?"

Our actor friend checked his watch. "I'm meeting my family in a few hours. I've never been part of a sting operation, either. I find myself really enjoying this. Do you mind if I tag along?"

Vance and I both shook our heads. When Michael stepped away to update his wife, my detective friend and I bumped fists together.

"We'll be telling stories about this one, won't we?"

Vance nodded. "You ain't just whistlin' Dixie, pal."

FOUR

Can you believe this is happening?" Vance asked, four hours later, as we both sat while a team of three assembled our costumes right before our eyes.

Now, I know what you're thinking. Costumes? Really? In this case, even though I know I went on record as stating I'd never be caught dead wearing a ridiculous getup in public, life will usually find a way to deliver a swift, brutal kick to the gonads when it feels like it. For me, it involved two women, both of whom appeared to be in their sixties, strapping various bits of metal to my chest, arms, and legs, under the watchful eye of the third. I then watched as three different battery packs were strapped to my body and either tucked away under my costume, or else disguised as another part of my outfit. What was I wearing?

One Mandalorian suit of armor.

For those of you who don't know what that is, it's a full-sized, *concealing,* instantly recognizable suit of armor from a very popular line of space opera movies. My armor, in essence, said I was a bounty hunter. The helmets worn by Boba Fett and Din Djarin, while not quite the same, had to be one of the single most recognized images in the *Star Wars* universe. Michael, who was sitting in a chair behind me, chatting with one of the people getting me outfitted, had called in some serious favors. I don't know how he arranged it, or what he had to promise, but a screen-worthy suit had been drop-shipped to us less than half an hour ago. This particular suit must have already been packaged up and ready to go because whomever Michael talked to had to have rushed it to the airport to make the two-hour flight north. In just over three hours, we had the armor, and it was taking nearly a full hour to figure out how to put the blasted thing on.

I watched as shin and thigh guards were buckled in place, and then my shoulder pauldrons were attached. The breastplate was next. Once I was properly outfitted, I caught sight of Sherlock and Watson watching me.

"Hi, guys. What's the matter? Don't like the costume?"

Both corgis head-tilted me, as though they were letting me know that yes, it sounded like me, but *no*, it didn't look like me. I heard a commotion on my right. Together, the dogs and I checked on Vance, who was in the process of being fitted for his own costume.

"If anyone ever hears of this, then I'm never gonna live it down," my detective friend mumbled.

I eyeballed the star-spangled leather outfit Vance was

wearing and gave him a thumbs up. While not necessarily spandex, the recognizable, patriotic-themed costume looked skin-tight, and the white star on his chest sparkled as though it was embedded with tiny crystals.

"Can't wait to see you in your mask, Captain," I snickered.

"You'd better not be filming this," Vance scowled. "Hey, where's your outfit? Shouldn't you be dressed up, too?"

Michael shook his head. "I come to these things to get noticed. That wouldn't happen if I wore something that concealed my identity, would it? Besides, you're the ones who need to go undercover. I don't, do I?"

"You're having the time of your life, aren't you?" I asked, suppressing a chuckle.

"Seeing the look of discomfort on both your faces has made my day," the movie star admitted. "You have no idea what it's like to sit in a makeup chair for hours on end."

"And you do?" I countered. "I don't recall you ever taking on a role in which it was necessary. Costume maybe, but not makeup."

Michael shrugged. "Costume, makeup, or prosthetics, it's a pain any way you look at it."

I rolled my eyes. "Yeah, sure. Rough life."

Michael grinned at me and pointed at the helmet. "Put it on. Let's see how it looks."

Once my outfit was complete, and I was looking at the outside world through the narrow slit in the helmet, I had to grin. If you would have told me last month, that not only would I be wearing this getup, but doing so in the presence of the original Kyle Reese from *Terminator*, I'd have labeled you insane. But, here we are.

Michael pointed at a nearby mirror. "Now you look like the guy who murdered me."

Both Vance and I turned.

"Huh?"

"What was that?" Vance asked, at the same time.

"My character in the show. He went up against *him* and was blown away."

I *did* remember seeing that.

Vance approached, grumbling like a petulant school boy, and folded his arms across his chest. Captain America stood before me, complete with face mask and round shield strapped to his back. I held up a finger, signaling him to wait. This was a Kodak moment I *had* to get.

"Jerk," Vance scowled.

"Think of it as a way to preserve the memory of this occasion," Michael suggested. "Do you have kids?"

I held up two fingers. "He has two girls."

"Don't you think they'd like to see you in that getup?" Michael asked.

Vance grunted and didn't say anything.

I held my phone up and showed him the picture. A huge grin split my friend's face as he studied himself.

"Not bad. Not bad at all."

Michael clapped his hands together and held up a simple black backpack "Are you guys ready? I've got your demon book right here. And, Jennifer tells me tonight's event is sold out. There's a better than average chance the people who took my gun are out there somewhere."

I stood up and started reaching for the door. Michael blocked my way.

"You're forgetting something." He held up a long, cylindrical package. "If you're going to wear the armor, then you need to look the part. Here."

The coverings were discarded and I was suddenly looking at a long rifle with what looked like a tuning fork at the end of the barrel.

"His sniper rifle. Nice. Wow, I really look the part, don't I?"

"Speaking of guns," Vance said, as he stepped beside me, "I'm not stepping out there without my firearm. I just need to figure out where to put it."

I pointed at Vance's hip. "Just wear it like normal. Steve Rogers had a gun strapped to his hip in the first movie."

"You can't go to an event like this with a firearm strapped to your side," Michael said, frowning. "Think of the kids that are out there. Hell, *my* kid is out there."

Vance retrieved his Beretta, still in its shoulder holster. He slid the clip out and ejected the round in the chamber. Then, he looked at the black straps, shrugged, adjusted the buckles, and fastened it over his costume. I had to hand it to him. It fit into his patriotic theme quite well.

"No one is getting my piece out of its holster but me," Vance promised. "It's perfectly safe. I can still draw it at a moment's notice."

The round he ejected was added to his clip and then returned to the gun. He then reached into his front pocket and pulled out a small box. Opening it revealed a row of small devices no bigger than a wireless ear bud. In fact, now that I looked at them, I realized they were smaller. Vance selected one and slipped it into his ear.

"Oh, no way!" I exclaimed. My helmet was removed and I reached for the second device. "Are you telling me we'll be able to talk to each other while on the floor?"

"That's exactly right. I don't need to tell you how

expensive these things are, Zack. Don't lose it."

"I won't," I promised.

Michael nodded, knuckle-bumped my own fist, and opened the door, leading back to the convention. The instant the door was open, we heard the loud buzzing of what seemed like a thousand different conversations. I looked down at Sherlock and Watson.

"Are you guys ready for this?"

"I'm not," Vance said, sighing. He poked his head out of the door and looked around. "Oh, come on! Why in the world are there so many people here? Don't they have anything better to do?"

"These things are popular," I told my friend, as I made sure Sherlock and Watson's leashes were wrapped securely around my hand.

"Nerds. Ugh. Let's get this over with."

"Hey. I was a nerd when I was little. Come to think of it, I'm pretty sure I still am."

"Yeah, yeah."

We both stepped through the door and joined the crowds of people. Vance and I both got our fair share of looks as we slowly walked around the large auditorium. Everywhere we looked, we saw fans of practically every movie conceivable. Many of the superheroes were identifiable from the moment I saw them. Others had me shaking my head. I clearly didn't follow comic books enough to know who—or what—they were supposed to be. Then again, it really didn't matter. These people were here to have fun, and dress up as their favorite characters. Who was I to judge?

A father and his young daughter stepped directly in front of me. They were both wearing rudimentary costumes, made from construction paper and cardboard boxes. However, both were recognizable. I was looking at another *Star Wars* bounty hunter, and everyone's favorite green-eared foundling.

"Wow, look at that one, Darcy!" the father exclaimed. He picked his daughter up and hurried over to me. "The attention to detail is amazing! You look exactly like him! Who made your costume, pal?"

"It, uh, was provided for me," I said, realizing with a start that it was the truth.

"Tell them nicely done! Can my daughter take a picture with you?"

"Go right ahead."

Getting into the spirit of the moment, I struck a pose I had seen on the show. The girl squealed with excitement.

"What is she supposed to be?" I heard Vance ask. He was standing about ten feet away.

"She doesn't look familiar to you?" I quietly asked.

"No. Should she?"

"It's the baby that my character takes under his protection. And … you have no idea what I'm talking about, do you?"

"Not a clue. Geez, how many pictures are they going to take?"

The father finished snapping pictures and thanked me profusely. Wishing the two of them off, I motioned for Vance to follow me to Michael's table. Our job was to stay in sight of the book at all times, and what were we doing? Goofing around with the fans. Well, I was. Vance was just an observer.

We found Michael posing for photographs. I should also point out that his table was the busiest. Everyone, it would seem, wanted to get the famous actor's autograph. In case you don't know how these conventions work, actors will provide pictures of themselves and, for a price, allow you to meet with them so that they can personalize a photograph. Then, if you wanted to pay a little extra, the celebrity would pose for a picture or two. In this case, I saw members of the Justice League, the Avengers, and practically every character in between laughing and talking among themselves as they waited for their turn. Sitting next to Michael was his wife, who had her own fair share of fans and admirers. I was ready to ask about Dashiel when I remembered Michael telling me about his mother-in-law and how she had come along on this trip, presumably to watch over her grandson.

I glanced over at Michael and we made eye contact. He nodded once and returned his attention to a starstruck young couple. That's when I noticed the table directly on Michael's right had the borrowed book of the dead. I wandered over and saw that the replacement movie prop, namely the Necronomicon, had been set up next to him. I'm also assuming it was because he wanted to keep an eye on it.

"Do we have any other undercovers here besides us?" I asked, as I leaned against a wall nearby.

"For a convention like this?" Vance asked. "No. We don't have the manpower for an operation like … oh. Are you asking if Medford does?"

"Yes."

"Ah. They told me they have three officers here, dressed as regulars."

"Good. Hey, I don't see you. You wandered off?"

"Look at the opposite row of booths, and then look

about a dozen feet on your left. See me now?"

"Aww! You found a group of kids dressed up as the Avengers. How sweet is that?"

"Bite me. As it happens, their Captain America was sick today. They asked me to stand in."

"And you willingly did so? Aww, welcome to Nerd World, amigo."

"Nope. Don't you *dare* go there. Hey, here's a thought. Perhaps you should bring Sherlock and Watson over here."

"Huh? Why?"

"Your dogs are very well known around here. You know this. If someone sees a person walking two corgis, I'm sure they're going to think it's you. However, if they see them with me, then people will more than likely think I'm you."

"Meaning, I'll be known as the guy in the star-spangled tights."

"These aren't tights," my friend sighed. "Look, with the dogs over here, you'd be free to simply observe. With that outfit, no one will suspect it's you, and that you're keeping an eye on that creepy book."

"They are *so* tights. Okay, you've made your point. You take them for a bit. I can hang out here and watch the crowds go by."

Sherlock and Watson didn't have any objections. After all, I had just dropped them off with a group of high-schoolers, with Vance overseeing the entire group. My two corgis settled to the ground and promptly went belly up. Dogs. Just before I left, Vance held out his hand, holding something foreign.

"What's that?" I asked.

"I've been thinking. I don't want anything to hamper

us being able to communicate, so take a spare, would you?"

I shrugged and slipped it into my pocket.

"How's everything going?" I heard a female voice ask me, nearly thirty minutes later.

Turning, I came face-to-face with Jennifer. "So far, so good."

"I don't see your dogs. I would have thought you'd bring them."

"I did. They're on my left, just across the way. If you're gonna look, don't be too obvious about it."

"Oh, okay. Yes, I see them."

"How's everything going back there?" I asked. "There's been a good turnout here. I'm impressed."

"It's been going amazingly well," Jennifer admitted. "It's making me reconsider turning down invitations to the smaller cons."

"Not a bad idea. Have you or Michael seen anyone who looked suspicious?"

Jennifer nodded. "That's why I'm here. Michael wanted me to tell you to be on the lookout for Zeus."

"Zeus? As in, the Greek god, wielder of lightning bolts?"

"Yes. Michael thinks he lingered much too long around that book. Plus, I saw several others dressed similarly. They might be the ones who took the gun?"

"Okay, tell him we'll keep our eyes peeled."

"We really should be in contact with him," Vance said, in my earpiece. "You know what? Give her your spare so she can give it to him."

I tapped Jennifer on the shoulder, as she started to turn away from me. "Here. Give him this. Tell him it's exactly what he thinks it is."

Michael's wife broke out in a smile. "Oh, he's going to love this, isn't he? Especially if it's what I think it is?"

I tapped the side of my head, clinking my helmet.

Jennifer hurried off.

"Is that why you gave the spare to me?" I asked, in a low voice. "You planned on giving it to Michael?"

Vance's voice sounded smug. "Maybe."

"Testing, one, two three, testing."

"Hello, Michael," I said, as I turned to look at his table. "We hear you loud and clear."

"Brother, this is cool as hell!"

"Thought you might like that. Thank Vance. He's the one who thought of it."

"You have my thanks, buddy," Michael told Vance.

"Uh, any time, pal," Vance returned. "Now, what about Zeus?"

"He's the one we're looking for," Michael stated, matter-of-factly. "He … well, hello to you, too. Don't you look handsome? Who might you be?"

Vance and I both heard a young voice start talking. Either the microphone was too far away, or wasn't strong enough to pick up soft voices, but either way you looked at it, we couldn't hear anything. After a few moments, we heard Michael agree to a picture, and then he autographed a headshot of himself and gave it to the smiling boy.

"There you go. Sorry. As I was telling Jennifer, Zeus lingered much longer than necessary in front of that book. He then looked around, as if he was looking for increased security. Guys, I think it's him."

"Well, if anything happens, he'll be the first one we target," Vance assured him.

I know Vance will refute this, and I know he'd like to

forget it ever happened, but I have video proof that he was truly enjoying himself. Every time I checked on the dogs, I'd find Vance interacting with fans. At first, it was nothing more than a polite smile, and a quick picture. But, as time passed, he'd start joking with the other participants, voluntarily adopt superhero poses, and openly encourage passersby to come in for a photo.

"Let's not forget why we're here, pal," I told my detective friend. "As fun as that is, we have to keep an eye on the book. If something happens to it, then it's our butts on the line."

"Sorry. It's for a good cause."

"Mm-hmm."

"Heads up, guys," Michael's voice broke in. "This time, I have ... who's the god of the dead?"

"The Greek god?" I asked. "Hades."

"Right. Hades was just here. He lingered, just like his buddy did."

"Did you see the two of them together?" Vance wanted to know.

"No, not yet. But, they were both dressed in white robes. They must be together, right?"

I met Vance's eyes. "It's possible, I guess. Until we see them together, we can't assume anything. If we ..."

"No, wait!" Vance interrupted. "Hades just met up with Zeus. There's someone else with them, too. Female, wearing the same type of robes. I believe she's wearing some type of crown, too."

"A tiara," I said. "She must be Hera, Queen of the Gods. She's Zeus' wife. And sister, if you want to get technical."

"Sister?" Michael repeated. "I don't care who you are,

that's not okay."

"It's very popular in Greek mythology," I explained.

"They were just joined by another female," Vance reported. "This one has on a similar outfit. I have no idea who she's supposed to be. Zack, care to take a crack at it?"

"Is she blonde?" I asked.

"Yeah. How'd you know?"

"Aphrodite. There are only so many female goddesses. Athena, Artemis, and Persephone."

"What do we do?" Michael nervously asked. "Should I take the book and make a break for it?"

"No, nothing that drastic," Vance said. "We still don't know if the Greek gods are responsible. Wow. I just heard myself say that. Thank you very much for making me sound like a nerd."

"I agree," I added. "I've got eyes on them. So does Michael. Hey, wait. Have Sherlock and Watson done anything?"

There was a pause as I saw Vance look over at the dogs.

"No. They're still hamming it up with all these kids playing dress-up. You know what? Just for kicks, I'm taking their pic."

"The dogs haven't reacted," I reiterated. "It's not a corgi clue."

"Better safe than sorry."

Just then, we heard a few shouts. Then, more joined in. The corridors rapidly filled with costumed people. Some started shoving, while others tried to get out of the way.

"What's going on?" I asked.

"The dogs just woofed," Vance said, at the same time. "I have no idea what they're barking at, but I did take a couple of pictures. I'm sending them to you now."

"Thanks. Okay, that means whatever is going to happen is *about* to happen," I said.

"Nothing has," Michael argued. "I'm looking at the book. No one has touched it."

"Good," Vance's voice said. "Zack, would you check it out?"

"Sure."

I moved off, which wasn't easy. After all, I now appeared to be moving against the general flow of traffic. What had happened? Why would shouting cause people to head the other way? Had someone pulled a fire alarm? Maybe there was a bomb scare?

I needed information

Several booths down, I found the source of the commotion. Three of the vendors were shouting angrily at each other, each accusing the other of thievery. Something had been stolen? Had we misjudged the appeal of *Army of Darkness'* Necronomicon?

"It was my sealed, first edition copy of Star Trek's very first comic book!" one older gentleman cried. "I know it was you. You were looking at it earlier!"

"I was only admiring it," a second person insisted. He was much younger, in his thirties, and covered in tattoos. "If you recall, I handed it back to you."

"What about my frog?" a woman suddenly asked.

Confused, I turned to the third person. The lady was a woman about the same age as me, wearing an outfit from some type of anime film. Besides, in what context would a frog be considered valuable?

"It has actual screen time in those classic beer commercials!" the woman insisted, as if reading my mind. "It was the gem in my collection. I saw *you* looking at it last!

Give it back!"

"I don't have it!" the tattooed man snapped.

"Not you, *her*!" the woman insisted. She was pointing at a young girl in a cheerleader uniform. "

"I—I don't have anything!" the girl protested. She held up her hands. "Look, I'm not even holding a purse!"

"Zack, get back here, on the double!"

That was Vance's voice, and he didn't sound pleased. Certain I was witnessing an orchestrated distraction, I snapped a shot of the arguing vendors and patrons and hurried off.

"Why? What's the matter?"

"Didn't you hear him just now? Michael said the book is gone! This shouting match I'm hearing? *That* was the diversion! Get your tail back here. The dogs are going ballistic!"

I hurried back to my friend, clinking and clanking worse than a newlywed's car fastened with strings of tin cans. I heard the dogs before I could see them. Both of them were barking their heads off, and that could only mean … of course! The person who took the book must be nearby! They were banking on the fact that everyone was in disguise, so that meant they were dressed up, too!

"They're still here," I reported, breathless. Hey, I never said I was an athlete. You try wearing forty pounds of metal strapped to your body. "Give me the dogs. We've got to find them!"

"Go!" Vance ordered, tossing me the leashes. "Get after them! I'll inform Michael."

"Where is he?"

"I think he's looking for the Greek gods. I'll go help him."

"Roger that. Sherlock? Watson? Find whoever took the book, okay?"

Sherlock and Watson let out a few piercing barks. Not the kind of barks that were designed to get your attention. Oh, no. These were the kind that said, *hey, we may be little, but we'll still take your feet off at the ankles.*

This time, I didn't have to fight the oncoming traffic. The dogs pulled me into the throngs of people milling about, trying to see what was going on. Sherlock, taking the lead, deftly wove around various obstacles, including people, chairs, walls, and so on. Me, in my clunky sci-fi armor, struggled to keep up with them.

"I'm sorry, ma'am. Coming through. No, don't mind me. I'm … what's that? Yes, they're cute, but insistent. When they get wind of something, they … my apologies. I'm just following them."

I counted. I ended up giving out at least twenty apologies. Thankfully, no one was offended, or tripped up, and we arrived at the main entrance. Sherlock turned to look back the way we had come.

"Oh, come on. You're not gonna make us go back through that, are you?"

I was ignored. The corgis were seemingly staring at a small group of people headed directly for me. As they neared, one of them, wearing a long, trench-coat style green jacket, a red baseball cap, black glasses, and a dark gray backpack, came to an abrupt stop. The character spun on his heel and immediately headed in the opposite direction.

"Vance? Are you there?"

"I'm here. Whatcha got?"

"Sherlock and Watson brought me to the door as

quickly as possible. We beat the guy here, so he couldn't leave. He's headed back to you."

"You saw him? That's beautiful! You rock, Zack! Which one is it? Zeus or Hades?"

"Neither. This one looks like Data, from *Goonies*."

"I have no idea who that is."

Oh, crap on a cracker.

"You need to get out more. Umm, he's …"

"I know what he looks like," Michael's voice cut in. "I just watched that movie with my son the other day. You're talking about the kid with all the gizmos?"

"Yes! That's him."

"I see someone like that heading this way."

"Where?" Vance demanded.

"Do you see the girl with the white hair?" Michael's voice asked. "She's got on black leather thigh-high boots."

"Wearing an outfit I'd never let either of my daughters wear?" Vance inquired.

"That's the one. See the guy with the green duster next to her? *Him*."

"He knows we're on to him," I reported, bringing up the rear. "He's changed direction again."

"I've alerted MPD," Vance said. "Their guys are converging. They … look out! He's making a break for it!"

The thief let out a cry of alarm and bolted for the front door. However, the dogs and I were already there. I was spotted, and he reversed course one more time. Without bothering to watch where he was going, he immediately sprinted away, no doubt to try and ditch the costume so we couldn't follow. What he didn't take into account was Vance's proximity. The thief managed to cover about ten feet before he came to a stop. The reason why? Vance, holding his shield in much the same way as the character he was portraying, had stepped directly into our suspect's line of sight.

There was a loud *CLANG* as the perp made contact. Vance's costume might be just that, a costume, but apparently, the iconic shield was made of metal. My detective friend quickly pulled out a set of handcuffs, from who knows where, and snapped them in place. As for me, I hurried over to unzip the backpack the thief was wearing. Reaching inside, I found an assortment of items. One by one, they were placed on the ground before the handcuffed man.

One rather unremarkable comic book was placed on the floor. Then, a scarred, decrepit green plastic lump joined it. I remember seeing the commercials which featured frogs croaking out the name of the beer company, but I sure don't remember them looking like *that*. Whatever. Last to be placed on the ground was a heavy leather-bound book with a grotesque face carved into its features.

"This can't be happening!" the incarcerated man sputtered with rage, as Vance pulled him into a sitting position. "How did you find me?"

FIVE

Thirty minutes later, I was back at what was starting to feel like my second home, which was Interview Room #2 at PV's police station. More specifically, I was sitting in a chair, watching Vance and a second detective interrogate the prisoner. In case you were wondering why we were back in Pomme Valley and not at the Medford police station, well, that was due to a little persuasion from one instantly-recognizable actor. If ever there was such a thing as a smooth talker, it'd be Michael.

He waltzed in, shook the hands of every Medford cop that he encountered, and sat down with their captain to explain why he'd like to see the case about his stolen property moved to PV. I don't know what was said, but as soon as they emerged from their closed-door meeting, Captain Ryerson announced that this particular case would now be a collaboration with their two departments. He even assigned Amanda Cartez, a Medford detective we had previously collaborated with, to the case alongside Vance.

With that said, our suspect was now being interrogated by both Vance and Detective Cartez, and from what I've been able to witness, it wasn't going too well. The interviewee did not appear to be intimidated in the slightest, and therefore remained tight-lipped. The only thing worth noting was that Vance was doing a remarkable job in keeping his cool. So far.

Over and over, he and Detective Cartez peppered the suspect with questions. Yet, no matter how much they tried, they couldn't crack the stoic demeanor presented to them by the prisoner. He just sat in his chair, looking dead ahead, with dull, vacant eyes.

"We're getting nowhere," I heard Vance say, which caused me to look up. "Do you think we're hicks? Or that we don't know what's going on?"

The tiniest of smiles appeared on the perp's face. His arrogance was driving *me* nuts and I wasn't even the one in the room with him.

"You stole that book with the intent of selling it to the highest bidder," Detective Cartez was saying. "You also stole the gun from that sci-fi movie. Where is it? This will go much better for you if you just cooperate."

A full-blown smirk appeared. Was he finally ready to talk?

"Come on, kid," Vance said, as he pushed back from the table in his chair. "Baby steps. Let's start with a name. Who are you? Who are you working with?"

They were met with silence. That was when the door opened in my room, admitting Captain Nelson and the lanky form of senior officer Derek Jones.

"Anderson. Any progress?"

"Not since the last time you were here. The little punk thinks he's smarter than everyone and that by shutting up, he'll remain a John Doe."

"He very well could," Captain Nelson sighed. "I've got the entire station trying to identify this guy. They're checking everything: federal and international databases, and even social media. I've left instructions to let me know the instant we have something."

Voices rose. I turned my attention to the interrogation and saw that, unfortunately, Vance's professionalism was starting to slip. My detective friend had become so irritated that his face was beginning to turn red. Detective Cartez looked as though she was ready to smack the smile off of the suspect's face.

"He's playing them both," I observed, using a low voice. "Our perp is the only one who is now calm and collected. Look at him."

"He does, and he isn't," Captain Nelson said, scowling. "I need to know how to make this guy sing. I want to crack him like an egg. Any suggestions?"

I was about to shrug when I caught sight of John Doe's smirk again. An idea formed.

"What?" the captain demanded. He had been watching my face, so he knew I had thought of a suggestion.

"His arrogance."

"What about it?"

"Use it. That's his weakness. He's smug; defiant. Well, use what we know against him. Egg him on! Laugh at him.

Vanity is a powerful weapon."

"How?" Captain Nelson asked.

"Get him angry. Provoke him. Everyone knows that when you're mad, you let things slip."

The captain pointed at the microphone. "Jonesy? Do the honors, would you?"

While Officer Jones relayed the idea to Vance, Captain Nelson leaned forward.

"How are your two Dog Wonders doing? I can't believe I'm saying this, but … corgi clues, have they found any yet?"

"A few," I admitted. "They're as unhelpful as they usually are."

"Will you tell me?"

"Sure. Let's see. The first was a picture taken at the comic con. There were so many distractions walking around that I have no idea what Sherlock and Watson were indicating. Then, some family walked by, and the dogs perked up. Again, nothing out of the ordinary. And the last? Just everyone's favorite detective, in the costume that was lined up for him."

The captain looked interested. "Oh?"

I showed him my phone. "What do you think?"

He snorted once and immediately reached for his glasses.

"That? That's Detective Samuelson? Send me that one, would you?"

"And he'll blame me for it," I said, shaking my head. "I'd rather not. However, you should be able to find it on the police department's social media page. I paid a kid ten bucks to correctly tag it, whatever that means."

"I'll do just that. Thanks, Anderson. Now, in the

meantime, take your secret weapons and find that damn gun, would you?"

"We'll do our best, Captain."

There was a knock on the door. It opened, and Julie Watt, my friend Harry's wife, poked her head in. She started to hand over a manila folder she was carrying when she caught sight of me.

"Hi, Zack! Captain, I thought you'd want to see this as soon as possible."

The captain put his thin wire-framed glasses back on.

"Thanks, Jules. Whatcha got there?"

"We have a hit on our John Doe."

Captain Nelson's eyes lit up. "No kidding. Excellent news. Hand it over. Let's see who we've got."

"There isn't much on him," Julie began, "but we do know that he's simply known as John Doe."

"John Doe?" the captain repeated. His frown deepened. "What kind of name is that?"

"He's managed to avoid being properly identified," I guessed. "I'm hoping there's some good news?"

Julie nodded. "Get this. He's a suspected member of the Hobbits of Highton!"

Captain Nelson leveled a stern look at the woman who had been cross-trained on so many office jobs that she could literally fill in wherever she was needed.

"The *what* of the *what*?"

"The Hobbits of Highton. They're a high-profile gang of thieves who are known for pulling off daring heists …"

"Never heard of them," the captain interrupted.

"… in Europe," Julie finished. "This is the first time a known member has been spotted in the United States."

"He's European?" I asked. "I wouldn't have called that."

"It's hard to tell, seeing how he won't say anything," Captain Nelson pointed out.

We watched Vance and the Medford detective throw insults around the room, covering every topic from questionable lineage to having an IQ so low that they'd have to dig to find it. A grimace appeared on our suspect's face, a fact which didn't go unnoticed by the captain.

"I'll be damned. Look, Jonesy. Anderson's idea is working. He's getting irritated."

"He sure looks that way, Cap."

"Well, what are you waiting for? Pass it on to Samuelson. And don't call me *Cap*."

"Sorry, Cap."

Captain Nelson was silent as he perused the files Julie had brought. Insanely curious, I tried not to be too obvious by preventing myself from reading over the captain's shoulder. I'd also like to point out that I'm pretty sure he took his sweet time reading the file.

"We suspected there was an accomplice," he finally said, a few minutes later. "Looks like we're right. It says here that this nerd fest usually travels with four members."

"What do we know about them?"

"We have a couple of pictures, but they're so blurry, or … what's the word nowadays? Pixelated? Whatever it's called, it's prevented us from getting a clear shot of these guys."

"And they're out of Europe," I said, taking a few of the pictures I was handed. "You're right. You can't make anything out on these. They could be wearing masks for all we know."

"They typically target small items. Easier to conceal. Swell."

"So this is the first time they were spotted in the States,"

I repeated. "Use that. Suggest they're slipping, especially since he was caught in such a small town as PV."

The captain nodded at Officer Jones, who immediately relayed the info.

"What's the matter, pal?" Vance was saying. "What does it say about you when you're snagged in a small town like this? You're not very good at this, are you? I'd be keeping ahold of your day job and stay in Europe."

"This *is* my day job," the young punk snarled.

"O-ho! He speaks!" Detective Cartez exclaimed. "What a revelation!"

"How did you find me?" the kid all but whispered. "No one has ever known I was there."

"You got greedy," Vance pointed out. "You swiped the gun and could've made tracks out of here, but nooo. You had to go back for seconds. Well, I hope it was worth it."

Inside the viewing room, the door opened again. Julie was back, only this time, a look of surprise had appeared on her face.

"Captain? You, er, uh, you're gonna want to hear this."

Captain Nelson rose to his feet. "I was just heading out. What is it?"

"We have some interest in Mr. Doe."

"Let's hear it."

"We have six different extradition requests."

The captain's eyes widened. "Six? From where, Europe?"

"No, that's what is so surprising. They all came from within the United States."

"Looks like our guy didn't get away as cleanly as he thinks," I said. "Sounds like they might not have been spotted, but they've clearly left their prints behind. Who wants him?"

Julie consulted her notes. "Henderson, Nevada."

"That's about fifteen minutes from Las Vegas," I said.

"Muncie, Indiana," Julie continued.

"About an hour from Indianapolis," the captain added. "Jules? Keep going."

"St. Petersburg, Florida. Then, we have Fort Worth, Texas. Tucson called next."

"Arizona," I said.

"And finally, we have a request from Metairie, Louisiana."

"Never heard of that one, I'm afraid."

"It's close to New Orleans," the captain said.

I held my hands up, in a time-out. "Wait. All six of these called in the last five minutes?"

"It's been more like ten," Julie corrected. "Once those prints were entered in, the calls started." She pointed at the flashing phone on the counter behind us. "I'm willing to bet that's number seven right there."

"Who was first?" the captain asked.

"Henderson."

He sighed. "And you told them we'd cooperate?"

"I did, yes. They said they'll drive up here, so we have some time."

"We have, at most, two days," Captain Nelson corrected. He turned to me. "Anderson, I want this case solved by then. You and your associates have *got* to find that damn gun. You follow?"

I nodded. "Completely. If you don't mind, I'll head to Jillian's and pick up the dogs."

"Agreed. You'd better get going. Jonesy? Break the news to Vance. Tell him to step on it."

Twenty minutes later, I was at Cookbook Nook. Sherlock and Watson were there, reclining on an armchair in the lounging area. Both looked up at me as I entered. Acting like they were doing me a favor, they rose to their feet, stretched, and jumped down from the chair.

"Who's watching you two?" I wondered aloud, as they both trotted over to me.

"That'd be me," Jillian announced, from behind a nearby book rack. "They're not going anywhere, at least, not without me noticing. I've got a tile floor in here. There'll be no sneaking around, thank you very much."

I rounded the corner and saw my wife sitting on the ground, with a stack of cookbooks in her lap.

"Hey down there. Whatcha doing?"

Jillian looked up at me and smiled. "Hey, yourself, handsome! Oh, just trying to untangle the mess a group of elementary students made in here. I found several stacks of books and am just restoring some order. How'd it go at the station?"

"He's not saying much, but they did manage to identify him."

"Oh, that's good to hear. What is his name?"

"John Doe."

"Yes, him. What's his name?"

"That *is* his name. Or, rather, what he goes by."

My wife sighed. "That doesn't tell us much, does it?"

"Quite the contrary. They've learned enough about him to have me do some searching. Oh, and I've got a deadline: two days."

"What happens in two days?" Jillian wanted to know, as she slid two books onto the shelf in front of her.

"Nevada cops will arrive and take our suspect back

with them. That is, unless one of the other five don't get here first."

"They're extraditing him? Wow. Do we know which city is requesting him?"

"Henderson."

Jillian shelved a book on a different shelf and held up a hand. I pulled her to her feet and stepped back.

"I've been to Henderson a few times," I admitted. "They've got a casino there with a large, smoke-free section, so that you don't end up smelling like an ashtray if you ever stop to try your luck gambling."

"I'm not a fan of the smoking, either," Jillian said. "Wait. Did you say there were five more states that want your suspect?"

"Yep. We may not know his real name, but we do know he's wanted. That's why I came back here. I was hoping to borrow your laptop and see what I can learn about a group of thieves who call themselves the Hobbits of Highton."

Jillian giggled. "A group of thieves call themselves hobbits? It makes you wonder, doesn't it?"

"Wonder *what?*" I asked.

"Whether or not they call themselves hobbits because they're small, or short. Anyway, feel free. My laptop is in my office. You can set it up by one of the armchairs, if you'd like."

I executed every type of search I could think of before throwing in the towel. Yes, I found some snippets of news here and there, but there wasn't anything that could possibly tell me who these characters are. Somewhere out there *must* be some more information, but who could I possibly ask for help?

"Is there something I might be able to help with?" a

familiar voice asked.

Looking up, I saw the smiling face of Michael Biehn, who was sitting in one of the chairs next to me.

"Wow. How long have you been there?"

"Just a few minutes. You appeared to be totally engrossed in whatever you're doing. Are you working on a story?"

"Believe it or not, I'm actually working on trying to find more information about the guy presently cooling his jets in a PV jail cell. Why aren't you at the convention?"

"Believe it or not, there is a schedule. I always allow myself some time to step away."

"And you came all the way over here?"

"I was thinking maybe I can help. I know a lot of people. Tell me what you're researching."

"The Hobbits of Highton. I figured Highton must be a place, so I started there. No luck. There are too many to list. Then, since so many states want to get their hooks on our guy, I figured there might be something newsworthy about the crimes they committed. Once again, nothing."

Michael blinked once and leaned forward. "What did you call them? Some type of hobbits? Isn't that a fantasy creature? It's a little person, right?"

"That's what I'm led to believe, too. Either we're looking for real life dwarfs or possibly some super short guys? I don't know."

Michael stroked his chin. By this time, it was well into evening, and a five o'clock shadow had appeared on his face.

"Your third option could be that this name is personal, and means something to them, so you might not ever find anything out online. Let's do this. We'll sic Jennifer on this. I wasn't kidding when I said we know a lot of people. And Jennifer, way more than me." Michael pointed at my notebook. "Write down the name you're looking for, would you?"

I did as requested, and slid the notebook over to the actor. Michael pulled out his cell.

"Jen, are you busy? Listen, I have a small favor. Well, *we* have a small favor. I'm sitting with Zack and he's made some progress on the case. The person who stole the gun is a member of a group called the Hobbits of Highton. We can't find anything out about them. Do you know of anyone who could help us? You need what? Hang on a sec. I'll put the call on speaker. There. Ask away, my dear."

"Zack? Are you there?"

I leaned forward. "Hello, Jennifer. Thanks for giving us a hand. What do you need?"

"What information do you have on this guy?"

I relayed what was known, including their name, types of crimes they typically committed, and the six states requesting extradition.

"We only have two days," Michael added. "Those states Zack mentioned all want their hands on him. Nevada is closest, and they are driving over."

"And if someone decides to fly over and get him?" Jennifer asked.

I looked at Michael and shrugged. "I guess they'd have to plead their case with Captain Nelson. From the sounds of it, he's already granted permission to Nevada. I honestly don't know how it works. If they don't get here in time, then he'll probably go to the second state that called."

"And if we solve the case first?" Michael prompted.

"Then that'd make the captain a very happy man," I

said. "He'd love to be the one who took this guy down."

"That should be more than enough," Jennifer decided. "I have several cop friends. Let me give them a call and I'll get back to you."

"Talk to you soon," Michael told his wife. He looked at me and gave me a lopsided grin. "If there's anything to be found, she'll find it. Or find a friend who can find it. I kid you not, she knows *everyone*."

The front door opened and a group of teenagers walked in, all girls. I'm guessing they were in high school, and clearly in some type of sports because each of them was wearing a red jersey with large white numerals visible front and back. The girls stopped long enough to give the dogs a pat on the head before they spread out to explore the store.

"How often do you get recognized?" I asked. "If you prefer not to answer, or think I'm asking too many questions, feel free to tell me to shut up."

Michael laughed. "Hey, it's not a problem. Um, I guess I'd say quite a bit."

"How many times have you been asked to say *come with me if you want to live*?"

"Thousands of times, brother. Thousands of times."

"Woof!"

Surprised, Michael and I looked down at the dogs. The corgis had just settled back to the floor after meeting the girls when both of them sprang to their feet and were staring in the direction they had gone.

"What are they doing?" Michael asked, using a quiet voice.

"They're alerting me to something," I replied, as I reached for my phone. "I don't know what, yet. One of the girls? Something they are wearing?"

"They're all wearing the same thing," Michael pointed out.

"Very true. Hmm, they've all gone in different directions. Sherlock? Watson? What are we looking for?"

Sherlock snorted once and turned to look up the stairs.

"What's up there?" Michael wanted to know.

"A little café," I answered, as I rose to my feet, prompting him to do the same. "And more books, of course."

"Want to head up there?" the actor asked.

I pointed at the dogs. "Thanks to the café, I can't bring those two up there. I ... look, a few of them are heading down the stairs. Let's just see if we can tell what the dogs are looking for."

A group of three girls passed us by, chatting animatedly among themselves. Two corgi necks swiveled to watch the small group go by.

"They're definitely watching them," Michael reported.

I snapped a few pictures of the girls. One was a blonde, one was a brunette, and one was African-American. What, exactly, was I supposed to be noticing here?

Michael's phone rang. "Hello?"

I heard Jennifer's voice.

"Well, that wasn't too hard. I don't know what search term you were previously looking for, but once I tried, I found all kinds of information about them."

"Wh-what?" I sputtered. "You found something online? Where? How?"

"She's very good on a computer," Michael offered. "She handles all of our social media accounts. So, what did you find out?"

"They're suspected in dozens of thefts," Jennifer

reported. "Everything they steal is presumed sold to private buyers."

"Did you find out what type of stuff they usually steal?" I asked. "Is it like Michael's gun? Are these movie props?"

"Each and every one," Jennifer confirmed. "They usually avoid big-ticket items, which in turn, helps them stay under the police's radar."

"And they only hit conventions?" Michael asked. "Lucky me."

"Conventions and a few private residences."

"Do we have confirmation that the stolen items end up in the hands of private collectors?" I asked. "I sure hope not."

"No, I'm sorry," Jennifer was saying, "I don't have that type of information."

"What about locations hit?" I asked. "Do they match up with the states where they're wanted?"

"That and then some. They're all predominantly smaller cities, which helps them avoid national attention. I'm guessing that's why you were having difficulties tracking them down?"

"Probably," I said, shrugging. "I don't suppose you found anything about the identification of their members? You said there were four, right?"

"Yes, there are four of them. Let's see. Again, this is all conjecture, but based on the P.I. friend of mine I asked, we're treating this as confirmed. Now, the rumored leader of the group is someone called Charlie. His trusted right-hand man is Danny."

"No last names?" Vance asked.

"None were given," Jennifer answered.

"How reliable is the information?" I wanted to know.

"My contact says ninety-nine percent sure."

"Gotcha. What about the other two?"

There was a pause. "These two names are classified as known accomplices. Whether they're part of the group or not is up in the air. I have last names for these two. Whether or not they're accurate, who can say? Ready? They're Alex Truett and Phoenix Jepsen. Both grew up in the same neighborhood as the one called Danny."

"It's a stretch," I decided, "but it's also a place to start. You've been incredibly helpful. Have Michael take you out to dinner tonight. In fact, go to the Chateau, here in Pomme Valley. It's my wife's favorite."

"Would you and Jillian join us?"

Oh, crap on a cracker. Me and my big mouth. I *loathed* that restaurant. Why? It was simply too fancy, too elegant for my tastes. However, Jillian adored it.

"I'll check with my wife before I confirm, but I'm almost positive she'd love to go."

"Fantastic! Shall we say seven?"

"We'll be there. Umm, should I give directions to Michael?"

"We'll let the phone's GPS get us there. Michael is terrible with directions."

"I'll bet I could give him a run for his money," I chuckled.

Michael laughed, told his wife he was on his way out the door, and rose to his feet.

"Zack, it's been a pleasure. Keep me posted, will you? I'd love to hear that you guys solved this thing before turning over your guy to another state."

"You and me both."

Once he was gone, I decided a phone call to Vance was necessary. However, my friend beat me to the punch. My cell rang just as I pulled it out.

"Hey, Vance. Were your ears burning? I was just about to call you."

"You were? What … ? Forget about that for right now. We've identified John Doe! We got a hit from Interpol. Turns out, his name is Alex. Alex …"

"… Truett," I finished.

"What the …? How did you know that?"

"I see your information and raise you three additional names, including the leader of the gang."

"Say *what*? Are you kidding? How did you find this out?"

"Hey, you've got your ways, and I've got mine."

I passed along everything Jennifer had told me. Vance, in return, passed along the wonderful news that they had finally managed to get Alex's smooth demeanor to crack. Make that implode, actually. Once Vance had spoken Alex's full name out loud, the calm and collected thief sprang to his feet, spitting mad.

It was Vance's turn to sit back in his chair and smile.

"You should have been there, buddy," Vance told me. "Once he slipped up, he tried like crazy to get his composure back, but I could already tell it was too late. When I told the little punk that six different states were fighting to see who'd lay claim to him, he announced he wouldn't be extradited by anyone."

"He thinks he's going to pull off an escape?" I asked, incredulous.

"That's what he said. I said something along the same lines. I asked him about the gun, hoping I could get him to slip up, but no, he still refused to acknowledge he knew anything about the stolen movie prop."

"You should tell him you've identified the remainder of his gang," I suggested. "Tell him we'll have them all in custody before this is over."

"He keeps insisting he'll be free soon," Vance said. "I don't like it, Zack. The little punk was too smug, although I did manage to keep myself from making a face. I didn't want to let him think he was getting to me again. Oh! I didn't tell you the best part, did I?"

Intrigued, I sat back in the chair. I heard twin snorts of exasperation as each of the corgis reluctantly slid into down positions and gave me judgmental looks. I gave each of them a few scratches.

"Let's hear it," I urged.

"The gun is still somewhere in PV!"

I sat forward, interested. "Are you sure? How'd you get him to tell you that?"

"It was easy. I told him that we were actively searching the town for the gun, and it was only a matter of time before we found it."

"And what did he say?" I asked.

"Two words: *good luck*."

SIX

It was half-past seven Saturday evening, yet it felt like it was approaching midnight. Yawning profusely, Vance hit the signal and turned left, onto Fourth Street. After apologizing to Michael that we'd have to bail on dinner plans, Vance and I, along with the dogs, were slowly cruising through town, hoping against hope that Sherlock and Watson would be able to find something worth investigating. Yes, it was dark, and I know we wouldn't be relying on visual cues. Instead, I was counting on the dogs alerting us to something they picked up, whether via smell, or just their crazy sixth sense. That was why I decided to take Vance at his word, and assuming the stolen gun was somewhere in town, begin some old-fashioned detective work and hit the streets. Thus far, the dogs were too busy sawing logs in the back seat of Vance's Oldsmobile sedan.

"Anything?" Vance asked, as we rounded a bend in the road.

I looked at their royal canineships and shook my head. "Nothing here, I'm afraid. They're both asleep, and if I'm not mistaken, both are drooling on your seats."

"Eww, that's gross! Get them to stop, would you?"

"Your car is a pile of junk attached to four wheels, pal. What are you worried about?"

"It still runs, and it's completely paid for," Vance argued. "There's nothing wrong with my car."

"Do Victoria and Tiffany enjoy being picked up in this thing?"

Vance nodded. "Sure. Why would they have a problem with it?"

"I can't wait to ask them for myself."

"Mm-hmm. Listen, how close are you to releasing your next Ireland book?"

"*Spirit of Éire*? Well, as you already know, the story has been finished, and I submitted the manuscript to my publisher."

"Okay," Vance said, shrugging. "That really doesn't tell me anything. When will you find it at the bookstores?"

"Next month. Early, I think."

"And the price?"

"That part is out of my hands. Why do you ask? I know you can afford to buy it."

"No, it's not that. I was just wondering about the time frame. I know you said that you finished writing it a while ago."

"About two months," I said, as I checked the map I

was holding. "Turn right."

"Turning right," Vance repeated.

Once we were heading south toward town, my detective friend eased up on the gas pedal. After all, it would more than likely not look favorably on him if he was issued a speeding ticket by a fellow officer. At the moment, we were slowly cruising through the residential part of town, so that meant we had to be on the lookout for kids playing in the street.

"It takes time to turn the file I submit into a book," I explained, as we crept by the houses. For the record, neither corgi bothered to wake up. Sighing, we made a left turn, stopped at the next stop sign, then turned left again, taking us in the direction we just came from, only one street over. "Think about it. The text file I create is formatted to fit a letter-sized piece of paper. Are all the books released in that size? No, of course not. The books have to be formatted to fit whatever application it's been given to: e-book, print book, audiobook, and so on."

"And this is something you have to do each time you finish a novel?" Vance asked, incredulous.

"Not me, no. MCU takes care of it. All I have to do is write the story. They handle editing, proofing, cover design, and marketing. Why are you asking me this? Are you thinking about writing your own book?"

"No, it's nothing like that. I was just … well, that is to say, I …"

"Spit it out, pal. Just tell me what you're trying to say."

"This isn't easy for me to ask this," Vance admitted, after a few seconds of silence had elapsed. "It's just that, well, thanks to you and your book sales, you've pretty much taken care of the girls' college tuition, so I really should let this go. But …?"

I smiled as I realized what my friend was trying to get up the nerve to ask me. "Okay, now I get it. You want to know about the royalties from the sequel, aren't you? You're wondering whether or not I was planning on splitting the proceeds with you?"

My friend wouldn't look me in the eye. "Forget I said anything. I don't want to ruin our friendship over …"

"We're both riding this boat together," I interrupted. "This wouldn't be happening if it wasn't for you. The answer to your question is, of course I am. We both made a fortune from the first novel. This one? From what MCU has been indicating, the sequel is going to blow the first one out of the water."

"Holy crap, Zack. I don't know what to say to that."

"Just keep grinning, pal. We'll keep cashing checks as long as readers continue to buy the book. If you don't mind me asking, why is this coming up? You know I'd never screw you over, don't you?"

"I know that, buddy," Vance said, in a subdued tone. "It's a subject I don't like bringing up. I don't know how I managed to jump on this royalties boat with you, but I'm honored to be there. My family and I consider ourselves lucky."

"Lucky?" I repeated, scratching my chin. "I think of it more along the lines of a window of opportunity opened before us, we happened to notice, and we were smart enough to jump through. Wait a minute. Did someone say something to you about it?"

Vance clammed up once more. Knowing my small circle of friends, it didn't take long to come up with a name.

"Harry. Harry said something to you, didn't he?"

"He might've," Vance mumbled.

"He didn't give you hell, did he?" I asked, growing irritated.

"No, nothing like that."

I suddenly laughed out loud, which caused the dogs to wake up in the back seat. Sherlock fired off a warning woof at me.

"Then, the opposite. He was complaining, wasn't he? Whining about all the money you're making?"

A smile formed on Vance's face. "Maybe."

I snapped my fingers. "So, that's what he's been doing. Oh, it's starting to finally make sense."

My friend looked my way. "What does?"

"Harry. Every time I see him, he's rambling on and on about some hair-brained idea of his. Don't you see what he's doing? He's trying to inspire me to write a story about one of his ideas. He's hoping I'll come up with something so that I'd be willing to share those profits with him."

"And has he?" Vance wanted to know.

"Hah. That's a laugh and a half, isn't it? Would you want to read a book about a talking iguana which undertakes a journey to save his family from a luggage factory."

Vance snorted with laughter. "No, he did *not* suggest that."

"Then there's last week," I continued, watching as Vance turned at the next intersection as we continued to canvass the city, "during lunch at Casa de Joe's, Harry told me about this dream he had, where the country was being invaded by intergalactic pirates, and that the ship they arrived on was a tall ship that could fly through the air."

"And you think Harry was trying to give you an idea for a book?"

"Why else would he say that to me?" I argued. "Does he ever tell you about something he's dreamt about?"

"Not once," Vance confirmed.

"There you have it," I said, laughing. "Poor guy. He probably thinks he's deliberately being left out."

"Would you ever consider another collaboration?" Vance asked.

"If the idea was sound, then yeah, of course."

"You'd better prepare yourself for a countless string of suggestions from him," Vance advised, chuckling.

"Swell."

Our search took us to the far eastern reaches of town. Vance shrugged and decided to expand our search, seeing how neither of the dogs had triggered on anything in the last hour. That is, until now.

"Awwoooo!"

"Ooo," Watson agreed, adding her low howl to Sherlock's.

Vance was so surprised that he immediately pulled over. The two of us twisted around in our seats so that we could see what the corgis were doing. In this case, Sherlock and Watson were resting their front legs on the left-hand arm rest and were looking out the driver's side of the car. What was out there? Just a few signs.

"What are we looking at?" Vance asked. In his eagerness, he had pulled out his notepad and was ready to take notes.

"Umm, it looks like advertisements for one of those fruit stands. I've actually been to this one before. They've got a pretty good selection of dried fruit. The apricots are really good."

The large billboard indicated Crozier Family Farms

was less than a mile ahead, on the left. I knew the dogs liked small pieces of fruit, especially bananas, but since I know those don't grow around here, I didn't have a clue what they could have, well, clued in on.

"What do you think?" I asked Vance. "Shall we go take a look?"

Vance looked at the dogs and shrugged. "Why not? It's not like they've shown an interest in anything else."

Once we were at the stand, and I had placed their canineships on the ground, they went full-on Clydesdales on me and yanked my sorry butt over to the counter. A young couple, probably very early twenties, had their backs to us and were busy arguing about something.

"I'm tellin' you, he won't do it," the man was saying. "You can't expect her to leave *him* for his brother. No one does that sort of thing."

"It happened last time," the woman insisted. "Sheila told me that Jerry and Dina ... oh, I'm sorry. I didn't see y'all there. Welcome! What can we get for you?"

"Sorry to interrupt your conversation," I began, offering the woman a smile, "but ..."

"Oh, heavens above!" the woman interrupted, as she leaned over the counter to stare at my dogs. "It can't be. Tell me you didn't just bring us Sherlock and Watson, the detective dogs!"

"Okay, I *won't* tell you that."

The woman's smile faded. "Oh."

"Wow, that was too easy," I chuckled. "Yes, it's them. Listen, how much longer will you be open?"

"We close at sunset," the woman reported. "I'd say you've got about half an hour. Should be plenty of time to pick somethin' out."

"Don't worry, everything looks great. I know I can find something to …"

I trailed off as I noticed both Sherlock and Watson were not staring at the girl, but at something behind her. If you're thinking they were staring at the man, you'd be wrong. He was now standing next to his wife, and the corgis were looking at something on the left.

"What is it?" Vance asked. "What are they looking at?"

"There isn't anyone over there," the woman informed us. "It's just me and my husband. Oh, where are my manners? I'm Elaine. This is Grant."

"Is this your farm?" Vance asked, still staring at the dogs.

"It belongs to my family," Elaine said. "Our entire family works here. Can I interest you in some strawberries? Maybe some fresh-picked apricots?"

"I'll take a flat of strawberries," I told her, as I pulled out my wallet. "And how about two pounds of the apricots? They smell fantastic. Hey, this might be an odd question, but can you tell what those two are looking at?"

Both Elaine and Grant leaned over the counter to stare at the dogs. Both turned in unison to see what was behind them. Then, they looked left.

"There's nothing here but what's left of our dinner," Grant said, shrugging, as he started tossing the leftovers into a brown paper bag. "It was too much, and I should probably just throw it …"

"Hold on a second, would you?" I interjected, and pointed at the dogs. "Keep holding that bag. Would you walk that way, to your left?"

Sherlock and Watson watched the friendly proprietor head down the counter.

"Now, come back here," Vance instructed.

Grant did as he was told. I pointed at the paper bag he was holding.

"They weren't looking at you before, but they are now. What's in the bag?"

"I told you, just what's left over from dinner."

"Believe it or not, this is important," Vance told the couple. "Please, what's in the bag?"

"Well, that bag back there has the potato salad and coleslaw. This one has chicken bones and some leftover potato wedges. There's no way I could eat all of it. You should see those wedges! It was like someone quartered whole potatoes and deep fried 'em. Sure are tasty, though."

Vance turned to me. "Potatoes? That can't be right. It's gotta be the chicken. What would they want with chicken? I mean, aside from the obvious, that is."

"Chicken," I murmured, thinking hard. "What in the world would they want that for? Maybe … maybe there's something about it? What kind is it? I mean, is it grilled? Fried?"

Grant shrugged. "It's fried. I know it's not the healthiest, but we couldn't help it. You should never ignore your nose."

"So very true," Elaine added.

"Fried chicken," I repeated. "What could …? You know what? I'll figure it out later. Smile, would you?" I took their picture. As if the dogs had been secured in place and I had just cut them loose, the corgis were immediately on the move. "Thanks, guys. We'll get out of your hair."

Shrugging, the husband and wife couple waved as we left.

"Stop by any time! And don't forget to bring your friends!"

"What's the deal with fried chicken?" Vance asked, once we were on our way.

"How do we know it's chicken? It could be potatoes. Or wedges."

"Hmm, that doesn't really help us."

"And not just chicken," I continued, "but fried chicken. I can think of a couple of things that could mean."

Vance eased up on the accelerator as we neared the outskirts of town. "All right, let's hear 'em."

"Well, think about it. Fried chicken. We might be looking for some type of religious angle."

"How the blazes did you go from fried chicken to religion? Not even Evel Knievel could make that jump."

"Church's Chicken? Ever hear of them?"

Vance's mouth snapped closed and he was silent for a few moments. "I hadn't even considered that. Well, along those same lines, we could be looking for spinach."

Enjoying the game, I sat back in the seat. "Popeye's. You're talking about Popeye's Chicken. Well, what else do we have?"

"Besides KFC? You'd have to consider every restaurant that sells chicken."

I shook my head. "No, I think it'd be places known for selling chicken."

"What a crazy clue," Vance decided. "Sherlock, Watson, give us something else, okay? What else do you guys have?"

The dogs were watching the passing scenery and ignoring us. Shrugging, Vance pointed at the first intersection as we entered town.

"You're the one who proposed we search the town using a grid-like pattern. We've made it through. What should we do, hit it again?"

I checked my watch. "We have time. I told Jillian we'd

be late. Sure, what could it hurt? Let's hit the main streets first."

Vance shrugged, and turned at the next stop light.

"You're taking us through downtown?" I asked, as I caught sight of a familiar row of buildings on either side of the street.

"You said to hit Main Street, so here we are."

"I said *main streets*, but what the heck, this is a good place to start."

"Woof!"

"Now what?" Vance asked, as he pulled over and parked. Much to my surprise, we were now in front of Cookbook Nook. "Sherlock, what's the deal? You want to go see Jillian, is that it?"

My tri-colored boy was, unfortunately, looking in the other direction, across the street. In fact, he seemed to be looking directly at Toy Closet, Woody's shop. Setting both dogs on the ground, Vance and I headed across the street to see why the corgis wanted to go in a hobby and toy store.

"Good evening!" Woody's voice rang out, as soon as we entered the store. "What can I ... hey, Zack! What brings you to my store today? I was just getting ready to close up. And would you look at that. If it isn't Sherlock and Watson! I'm sorry, guys. I seem to be out of treats at the moment."

"They get plenty of them," I assured him. "Woody, listen, can we look around in here? We're working a case, and we have a feeling there might be something in here we need to see."

Woody's smile disappeared. "I'm not doing anything illegal, nor am I selling anything I shouldn't be."

Vance shook his head. "What Zack meant to say is that the dogs were showing interest in the store. That means there's something in here they want us to see. It could be a figurine, or a pair of dice, or who knows what."

"Oh, you mean Toy Closet has a corgi clue somewhere in here? Why didn't you say so? Please, feel free to look around!"

"Did you hear that?" I asked the dogs, as I dropped the leashes. "What do you want us to see? Vance? Keep an eye on the door, okay?"

Vance nodded. "Got it."

Sherlock and Watson dropped their noses to the ground and started sniffing. Both moved past Woody's check-out station and paused as they inspected the three long aisles of racks crammed with models, toys, and a wide assortment of merchandise suitable for practically every hobby. Model rocket engines, custom pliers for making jewelry, coin albums for the budding numismatists, and even white gloves and tweezers for philatelists. While small, this little store seemingly had a little bit of everything.

The dogs moved to the farthest aisle on the right and trotted down it, as though they were shopping for a present. Sherlock stopped about halfway down and looked up at the stacks of items sitting on the shelves. He looked at Watson and, together, they sat.

"What do they see?" Vance asked, as we hurried over. "Wait, what's this? Games?"

"Board games," I clarified. "They stopped at a huge stack of classic board games. Check it out. Woody has a vintage Uncle Wiggly game. I used to play that all the time when I was little. Hey, there's Chutes and Ladders. That was another of my favorites. And Candyland? That'd be one of

Jillian's, although she claims she's got the worst luck."

"Isn't that game based on randomness of the colored cards?" Vance asked.

"You know it and I know it, only she doesn't. And, I have to admit that I think she's right. She lost a whopping fifteen games in a row once."

"You guys still play board games?" Vance asked, unable to hide the skepticism in his voice.

"Absolutely. I can't speak for her, but for me? It's nostalgic. It brings back tons of childhood memories. Well, can we tell which game they're fixated on?"

"Not unless we take each one of these out, one at a time," Vance replied, sighing. "Just take a picture of this section right here. I'm sure we can figure it out later."

"Uh-huh. Sure we can. Since when has that ever worked for us?"

Vance laughed and stepped out of the way as I snapped a few pictures. Their mission accomplished, the corgis rose to their feet, gave themselves a good shaking, and then sidled next to Vance. My detective friend shrugged, reached into an inside pocket, and produced two doggie biscuits.

"What did you guys find?" Woody asked, when we returned to the front of the store.

"Board games," I reported. "We don't know which one, since he was looking at an entire stack of games. We'll have to figure out which one he wanted us to notice later."

"Board games," Woody repeated. He shrugged and checked both of us. "Not gonna buy anything, huh?"

I started to sigh when I realized there *was* something I was meaning to check out in here.

"You have albums for collecting paper currency, don't you?"

"First aisle, about two-thirds of the way down, on the right. You a collector?"

"It's something Jillian just started for me. She found a monthly subscription where I receive five or six foreign bills a month. It's really quite fascinating, actually. I just received a few bills from Cambodia, and then one from Somalia."

"I have several albums available," Woody told me, growing excited that he now sensed a sale. "They range from amateurish to the leather-bound version with thick plastic pages."

"I've got an album already," I told him, "but I could use some replacement pages."

With my purchases in hand, we bid Woody farewell and headed on our way.

"Board games," Vance said, as we pulled onto Main Street. "I don't see how that could help us."

"We've seen stranger clues," I reminded him.

"True. Where should we try now?"

"Head to Third, then turn left. We didn't hit the southern part of town much."

We cruised by every house, every store south of Main, and were about to throw in the towel and head back to the station when Vance and I heard music to our ears.

"Woof!"

"What's he got?" Vance asked, as he looked for a place to pull over.

"I don't know," I admitted. "I must've missed it when he explained what he was looking at."

"Aren't you a barrel of laughs?"

I shrugged and gave my friend a smile. "Hey, that's me. I'm hilarious."

"Uh-huh. Jerk. So, what's over here?"

I checked the surroundings, looking for some indication of where we were. Vance parked the car and the four of us clambered out.

"Alright, we're at the corner of Third and Pine. Downtown is only a few minutes away, so we're still well within city limits. Guys? Where do we need to look?"

"Awwooowooo."

"There's something about those low howls of his that makes me laugh," Vance chuckled. He walked behind Sherlock to check which direction he was looking. "It's gotta be that building over there. The three-story Victorian? See it?"

"It's rather hard to miss," I said. "Sherlock? Watson? Let's go see what it is, okay?"

"I think it's a hotel," Vance said, as he hurriedly crossed the street. "Yeah, see the sign? Quinton's."

"It's a B&B," I corrected. "Quinton's Bed and Breakfast, to be precise. Guys? What do you want with this place?"

As usual, I was ignored. The dogs pulled me up the short flight of steps to the landing just outside the main entrance. Entering the lobby, the first thing either of us saw was the large oak, live-edge counter running the length of the room. Two work stations had been set up, much like the counter at a bank. The lobby had a travertine tile floor, gold-framed prints on the wall, and a crystal chandelier overhead, centered in the room.

This had to be the nicest B&B I had ever seen. A middle-aged woman behind the counter looked up as we entered.

"Good evening! Welcome to Quinton's Bed and Breakfast. How can I assist you today?"

I had adequate time to respond, only I wanted to wait and see if she recognized the corgis. And, I wasn't disappointed.

"Oh, for heaven's sake. I know these two! Would they be Sherlock and Watson?"

"They are," I confirmed.

"And you're Zachary Anderson! Well, I'll be! What a pleasure to meet you! What brings you to our establishment?"

I pointed a finger at the dogs. "Them. There's something they want us to see in here."

"Oh. Goodness, gracious. Do you know what that might be? What could you be looking for here?"

Vance and I eyed each other. My detective friend stepped up to the counter.

"Detective Vance Samuelson, PVPD. I don't suppose you could tell me who you have staying here at the moment, could you?"

"Not without a warrant," a male voice said. An older man, wearing a gray short-sleeve collared shirt, blue jeans, and black cowboy boots, emerged from a closed door behind the counter. "We respect our customers' privacy, and until you produce a warrant, our hands are tied."

A collar jingled. Looking down, I saw that Sherlock was staring at something on the right. A small dining room was there, with a rectangular wood table with seating for ... wow, that's a lot of chairs. Let me see. Twelve. There was room for a dozen people, but only two were there. Two young guys, one blonde, and the other with short, spiky black hair, had just risen to their feet and were heading for the counter to dump their paper plates and flatware into the trash. I checked the time on my cell. It was just past eight. Some people like to have dinner late. After all, I'm planning on doing the same tonight.

That was about the time when both Sherlock and Watson started barking like crazy, as if those two guys were aliens in disguise. Their heads jerked our way and saw the dogs. They took one look at us, zeroed in on Vance and the badge prominently displayed on his belt, and let out a collective cry of surprise. Both essentially leapt over the table using a type of fancy flip I've only seen in martial arts movies and darted out the door.

The corgis came very close to choking themselves. They wanted to pursue!

"What's with them?" Vance wanted to know.

I pointed at the door the two guys disappeared through.

"It must have had something to do with them. They took one look at us and bolted through that door. I'm starting to think that maybe, just maybe, they're the people Sherlock and Watson wanted us to find?"

"This may be a hotel, and not their own personal home," Vance mused, "but they still have their Fourth Amendment rights. I'd love to search their room, but I can't. Not without a warrant." He turned back to the male innkeeper. "You have a choice here, pal. I can go back and get my warrant, which, let's be honest, will take a little time. I'm going to tell you right now, that if we discover a certain set of thieves have been staying here, and you prevented us from checking out their room before they had a chance to clear it out, it's not going to go well for you."

"I knew you were going to say something along those lines," the owner said. His gruffness was gone. It looked as though the seriousness of the situation was sinking in. "Thankfully, I have a way for you to bypass your warrant."

Vance looked interested. "I'm listening."

"Checkout was at eleven. I know those two haven't renewed their stay with us. Yet. They kept saying they'd let us know when their final checkout date would be. I can say, with certainty, that the Fourth Amendment doesn't protect them now, since those rights expired after their paid checkout passed at eleven this morning."

"They don't know when they're going to be leaving?" I asked.

The owner nodded. "That's the impression I got. We had a problem like this a few years ago. We looked up what we could and couldn't legally do."

Vance pocketed his cell. "Beautiful. That works for me. I'd like a card for their rooms, please."

"We only have eight rooms here, but this key will open all of them."

"Which rooms were they in?" I asked.

"Room. Singular. They all shared it."

Vance's notebook appeared in his hand. "*All?* How many are we talking? By any chance, would that number be four?"

The female owner nodded. "As a matter of fact, it is. How'd you know that?"

"Which room?" Vance asked, ignoring the question.

"Number seven. It's on the second floor, all the way at the end. You can use those stairs through there."

The four of us headed up. Well, two of us did. I held Watson, and Vance carried Sherlock. The corgis could've handled the stairs themselves, but sometimes it was just easier—and quicker—to carry their Royal Canineships.

"Here we go," Vance announced, as we approached the end of the hallway. He held the key card up to a small sensor plate and was rewarded with a loud click as the door unlocked. "Pomme Valley police. Who's in here?"

We were met with silence.

"I think we caught them unaware," I said, as we stepped into the room.

There were two queen beds against the far wall. We could also see a small, folded cot propped up in the corner and a lump of vinyl next to that. An inflatable mattress, perhaps? On the two beds were two open suitcases, three duffel bags, and something that looked like a large orange tackle box.

Vance tossed me a pair of gloves. Once we were sure we weren't going to leave traces of our DNA everywhere, we started poking around. The first thing I wanted to investigate was the big orange box.

"Wow, get a load of this!" I whistled, as the box was opened. Several folding trays extended, and I was suddenly looking at a very large collection of professional makeup.

Vance nodded. "Those nerd fests. People like to play dress up, and sometimes you have to look the part. Besides, that's nothing. Check this out."

My friend had pulled open one of the duffel bags. Inside was a selection of wigs and hair accessories that would make a spy proud. We found hair in every length, and in every color of the rainbow. That was just the first bag. The second held a selection of clothes and hats: jackets, shirts of all styles, including long-sleeved, business, and tees, were there. Oh, we mustn't forget the shoes. We found styles for every occasion. Business, casual, formal, boots, sneakers, and so on.

We moved to the two large suitcases that were open on the bed. What we saw had us both gasping with surprise.

What was in them? Costumes. I saw uniforms from at least a half-dozen different shows covering the last five decades, including both television and film. I recognized a popular space travel show (you know the one I'm talking about), two costumes I recognized from a well-known space opera series, and one I recognized from a show in the nineties. The last two were familiar, but I couldn't place them.

"I think you're right," Vance was saying. "We've hit the jackpot here."

"This room was used by the Hobbits of Highton," I said, almost reverently. "I wonder how many people would like to get their hands on this stuff?"

"I'll let the captain know that we need to thoroughly tag and bag everything in here," Vance said, as he stepped outside to call in our discovery.

While he did that, I gave some slack in the leashes to my dogs and let them wander around. However, the only thing they did was take me straight to the sliding glass doors of the closet. Carefully nudging one aside, I gazed at what was on the three hangers and made a realization. I knew that outfit. I mean, I should. I just saw it at the convention yesterday. There were cameras everywhere. I'll bet we could get a good visual on our *hobbits* just by looking for people wearing the outfits in this room.

"The captain is thrilled," Vance reported, as he returned to the room. "Whatcha got there? Find something good?"

I pointed at the costume. "We've seen this before. I think if we check the footage, we can get a physical description of this guy."

Vance surveyed the contents of the suitcases. "We can probably identify all of them if we look for these costumes."

"My thinking exactly."

"Any sign of the gun?" Vance asked.

I looked down at the dogs. Sherlock and Watson were now ignoring me, which typically told me that they had shown us everything there was to see in a crime scene.

"It doesn't look like it, or else they would have found it by now. I think we've seen everything we need to see."

"The captain wants to …" Vance's cell rang, cutting him off. "Detective Samuelson. What's that? Oh, he does, does he? Beautiful. We'll be right there."

"What is it?" I asked, when Vance terminated the call.

"Our guy, Alex. They told him we found their room. Suddenly, he wants to talk."

SEVEN

Well, here I was. Again. I could complain, but seeing how I wasn't on the receiving end of all the questions, I really didn't want to tempt the Fates. It also didn't help that all the police officers knew me by sight, and didn't bother questioning why I was back yet again. Then again, it could have something to do with the fact I had Sherlock and Watson with me. I've said on numerous occasions that my two dogs will always be more famous than me.

"Welcome back," the girl manning the front desk said. "Just head on back. I know Detective Samuelson is already in the interrogation room with your suspect."

"Number two?" I asked, as I let the dogs guide me around the counter and toward the hallway.

"Yes."

"Is there an interrogation room number one?"

The woman nodded. "There is, but it's used for storage."

"Ah. Guys? Shake a paw, would you? I don't want to miss anything."

We navigated our way through the back hallway, which deposited us into the heart of the station. Several rows of desks were laid out, and a quick glance confirmed nearly half were occupied. Most of the cops had something nice to say to the corgis as they passed. However, there were always a few who looked down their noses at the dogs. Strange behavior, if you ask me. After all, we were on the same team. Then again, it must be a bitter pill to swallow when a pair of adorable dogs manage to solve more cases than the entire police force combined.

We had just passed Officer Jones' desk when the dogs pulled me to a stop. As one, they turned to look right. An officer I wasn't familiar with was sitting at one of the desks, poring over a report. The corgis pulled me up to the officer's workspace and promptly sat.

"Not everyone has treats for you two," I reminded the dogs.

The young officer looked up. He was in his early twenties, had short brown hair, and wore thin wire-framed glasses. He quickly rose to his feet and held out a hand.

"Good evening, sir. Officer Mason Riley. Would you get a load of that! Corgis! Wait. Are those two Sherlock and Watson?"

"They are," I confirmed. I really wasn't paying too much attention to the policeman. I was, instead, focused on trying to figure out why the dogs had dragged me over here. *And*, both dogs sat, which meant there was something here I was supposed to see, but what?

"Of course! That means you're Zack Anderson, aren't you? I've heard so much about you!"

"Good things I hope," I said, smiling. "It's good to meet you, Mason. I don't think I've seen you before. Have you been here long?"

"This is my first week here," the officer proudly proclaimed. "It's why I'm working the late shift. I started last Monday. I was working at Klamath Falls, but my wife pushed me to apply here when a position opened up. We have family here."

He turned to his desk and picked up a photograph of a smiling young woman holding a squirming boy of about two.

"Is that your family?" I asked.

"My wife, Sheila. That's my boy, Martin."

"You've got a great looking family," I told the new hire. "You're a very lucky man. I ..." That's when I caught sight of *what* the boy was holding. "Mason, tell me something. Your son, Martin, is it? What's he holding?"

"Oh, that? It's his favorite toy. He won't ever put it down. And, since he likes them so much, I've become an expert. This is one of the good guys, and is called Bumblebee. They're known as ..."

"... Transformers," I breathed. "I'll be a monkey's uncle."

"Is something the matter?" Mason asked.

I pointed at my dogs. "Would you do me a favor and pick up that picture? Great, thanks. Now, would you move it to the opposite side of your desk? If I'm right about this, the dogs are going to watch you as though you were holding a huge spoonful of peanut butter."

"They're watching me," Mason confirmed. "It's kinda creepy. Why are they doing that?"

"It would take too long to explain. I'll let the others fill you in. Now, watch what is going to happen. With your permission, I'm going to take a picture of that picture. When I do, both dogs are going to break out of their trance and probably head on their way."

"Really?"

"Just watch. There we go, picture taken."

Sherlock and Watson rose to their feet and were pulling me in the opposite direction, anxious to get going.

"That's really …"

"… interesting?" I offered.

"… strange," Mason decided.

I thanked the officer, assured him that around the station, the dogs' behavior was quite normal, and hurried to catch up to the dogs.

It says something when you're at a police station so often that you don't need to ask for directions on how to get to the observation side of interrogation room number two. People smiled and nodded as we passed, police and civilian alike. In fact, we were stopped three different times, since the police men and women loved to interact with the dogs. Doggie biscuits were produced, corgi derrieres hit the ground, and we ended up being delayed for so long that, by the time we arrived, Vance had already started the interview with our suspect, Alex.

"Did we miss anything?" I whispered, even though I knew full well the room was soundproof.

Captain Nelson looked up as the three of us walked in. He immediately patted his pockets, as though he was searching for a bag of doggie treats. For the record, I have *never* seen him carry them before.

"Anderson. No, not really. They just started a little bit ago."

"Good. I don't want to miss this."

The captain nodded. "You and me both."

"We found your disguises," Vance was saying, "and we found your clothes. Do you know what I don't believe?" He fell silent for a few moments, in case Alex wanted to say something. As it was, he didn't. "Why is it so many states are looking for you guys? I actually thought you guys might be good at what you do, but here you are, in a dinky little town in Nowhere, Oregon, and we not only have you, but we also have all the stuff your gang had. It's kinda disappointing, if you ask me."

"I wasn't," Alex quipped, in a quiet voice.

"Pathetic, even," Vance continued, ignoring the fact that his suspect had actually spoken. "I figure we'll have the gun returned to the rightful owner in, what, less than twenty-four hours? Sound about right?"

"You'll never find it," Alex said. His voice was low, and it was emotionless.

"We found you, didn't we?" Vance countered. "And, we weren't even trying. What happened when we started to look? We found your room at Quinton B&B."

"That wasn't you," Alex snapped. "It was those two damn dogs. If you didn't have them, you never would have found us."

Delighted, Vance grinned at the sulky face opposite him and sat back in his chair.

"So, you're familiar with Sherlock and Watson? Trust me, pal, they've solved way harder cases than what you present. They've solved hundred-year-old crimes, located murderers, and, obviously, found items that had been stolen. You, kid, don't stand a chance."

The smirk was back. "We'll see. You were lucky. You found us once. It won't happen again."

"It will when we get those dogs involved."

A scowl appeared, but only for a moment. Vance noticed and pounced on it.

"You're afraid of those dogs, aren't you? Well, you should be. After all, they found you *and* they found your room. Plus, we now have all of your gear, your clothes, and your disguises. That's gotta stink, doesn't it? And, I'm willing to wager that what freaks you out the most is you don't know how the dogs did it. Admit it!"

"I admit nothing."

"Vance is right," I said. "Our friend Alex is worried we'll find the gun. And do you know what? He's right. We're going to find it."

"Glad to hear it," Captain Nelson said. "Personally, I'd like to get my hands on the rest of them."

"Based on the amount of clothing and makeup we found in that room, they could, unfortunately, be anyone."

"But you said two of them were scared off," the captain pointed out. "That implies they don't have any way to change their appearance."

"Yet. But, that doesn't mean they can't go out and buy some new clothes, or makeup, for that matter."

"True."

"And the two we saw? Who could tell if they weren't already wearing disguises?"

"A fair point, Anderson."

Back inside the interrogation room, my buddy Vance

was having a field day. His smile widened.

"When would you like to tell me about Uncle Pennybags?"

I have to admit that the kid, either late teens or early twenties, could have been a professional actor. He genuinely feigned innocence and said he didn't know anything about an uncle.

"He's the character featured in Monopoly," Vance explained. "The old man? We found the black suit, top hat, and monocle mixed in with your things. The mustache was there, as were the phony bags of money he was carrying when we first spotted him yesterday. It was all there, so there's no point in denying it. We confirmed it with the security footage. That means one of you were there, so logic suggests that all of you were, too. So, who was the old man? Out with it. Was it you? Or ..." I watched Vance pull his notebook and flip through a few pages. "... Charlie? What about Danny, or Phoenix?"

For the second time, Alex's calm visage slipped. A look of panic appeared, but just as quickly disappeared.

"Who?"

"He caught that, right?" I asked, as I turned back to the captain. "Did you see it? Alex was surprised. He had no clue we knew the names of his companions."

"I saw it," Captain Nelson confirmed. "Samuelson noticed, too. Look. He's staring at the kid as though he just sprouted wings. He's not buying it, either."

"Surprised?" Vance was saying. "Didn't see that coming, did you? Oh, it's amazing how much you can learn when one department collaborates with the other. You see, Alex, we know all about you. We know you target these types of conventions and look for small, but profitable, targets. That must mean you already have a buyer lined up for that prop gun, isn't that right?"

A scowl appeared on Alex's face.

"Listen, either start cooperating, like you said you were going to, or I'm gone. If you're half as smart as you think you are, you'll start talking. Otherwise, adios! Well? Nothing to say? Suit yourself."

I watched Vance slowly gather his papers together, tap them a few times on the counter to align them, and slide them into a folder. He nodded once at Alex and rose to his feet.

"Okay!" Alex cried. "Fine, you got me, okay? Whadya want to know?"

"That's easy. Where's the gun?"

"I don't know, man. I didn't take it. I don't know where it was stashed."

"Who's the one who stole it?" Vance asked.

"Phoenix."

"Tell me how he did it."

Alex shrugged. "No idea. None of us know how the other does it. Those are the rules. Phoenix said he could handle the mark. All the rest of us had to do was distract."

"Who handled the approach?" Vance asked, as he twirled his pen around his fingers.

Alex blinked. "Huh?"

"Don't play dumb with me, kid. Think you're the first con artist who's crossed paths with me? The approach. Who handled it?"

Alex was silent.

Vance closed his notebook. "Your choice. Good luck in …"

"Danny. It was Danny, all right?"

"What approach is he talking about?" I asked the captain.

"You should try writing a thriller," Captain Nelson chuckled. "The approach is where one of the players makes contact with the mark."

"In this case, the mark is Michael Biehn?"

The captain nodded. "Yes. The actor. Someone approached him, chatted with him for a bit, and was able to get a feel for what it was going to take to pull off the heist."

"He told me the gun disappeared so fast that it made him question whether or not he really brought it."

At Captain Nelson's encouragement, I found myself sitting in front of the microphone.

"Find out which one of them actually stole the thing," I relayed.

"Who made the hit?" Vance asked.

Alex hesitated.

"I can only assume that the three of you created some type of distraction large enough to get everyone's attention off that gun. I want to know who did what."

"It was Charlie's idea," Alex finally admitted. "He's an expert in human psychology."

"What does that have to do with anything?" Vance wanted to know.

"Charlie knows how people think," Alex responded. His tone suggested Vance was a dullard for asking for an explanation. "Herd mentality. When large groups of humans are together, they tend to act the same way at the same time. Charlie is a master at getting people to do what he wants without realizing they're doing anything in the first place."

"Didn't see that coming," I murmured.

"What was that?" the captain asked.

"Intelligence. I just figured we were dealing with a group of teenagers, or maybe some college kids. Alex is right. Herd mentality is real, and if used properly, could definitely make life easier—or harder—for some people."

"You want me to turn on my friends?" Alex suddenly asked, raising his voice. "Then, you'll have to make it worth my while. What's it worth to you?"

"What do you want?" Vance asked.

"What do you think? I have no desire to see the inside of a jail. Let's start there, shall we?"

"No deal," Vance said. "The American justice system is not going to look the other way, based on your record alone. Nice try."

"What if … what if I tell you where you could find the other three?"

"The other three *what?*" Vance asked, sounding innocent.

"You know what," Alex snapped.

"I need to hear you say it. The other three *what?*"

"Fine. The other three … *hobbits*. We've clearly underestimated you. You know who we are. Well, I know *where* they are. Now, what's it worth to you?"

Vance turned to look at the mirror.

"I don't have an answer for him," I said, turning to the captain. "What do you want to tell him?"

"That we can put in a good word to the prosecuting attorney. We can tell whatever state officials that show up here to claim this guy, he was cooperating and to go easy on him."

I relayed the info. Vance did the same after he heard

the captain's offer.

"I really don't have much of a choice, do I?" Alex said, sighing. "Fine. There's a brick building with a white top not far from here. It looks like a bell tower to me. That's where you'll find them."

"And you expect me to believe you?" Vance asked, not bothering to hide his skepticism.

"We always have an escape plan," Alex explained. "If something was to ever happen to one of us, then we'd all fall back and regroup at the agreed upon point."

"And that building is your fallback point?"

"Yes. Listen, I don't feel right about this. They're my brothers. They can be very vindictive. You'll be able to guarantee my safety, won't you?"

"I am *sooo* not buying this," I said.

"You and me both, Anderson," Captain Nelson grumped. "This guy is jerking us around. We'll get to the bottom of this. You might as well take off. I need you and your secret weapons to go hunting, know what I mean? My officers will investigate this claim about the courthouse. As for you, use your dogs to find the others. I expect you'll have better luck than we do. Now, listen to me carefully. Don't engage, and certainly don't approach. If you happen to come across one of them, call it in, understand?"

"You got it. Sherlock? Watson? That's our cue. Let's go, okay?"

Five minutes later, we were back in my Jeep. I had pulled away from the station and called my wife to let her know I was going to head home when I found out that she was at Cookbook Nook. Her store may close at nine, but since I was working, she decided to work, too. Therefore, I turned on Main and parked in front of the store. Based on the day I was having, it'll be good to see her smiling face. Jillian always manages to help calm me down and think more clearly.

The dogs and I walked up to the main entrance of my wife's store. A group of customers were approaching us from the inside, intent on leaving, and I automatically pulled the dogs to the side, allowing them to pass. Once they had, I took a few steps toward the main counter, where I could see my wife chatting with one of her employees, when my arm was violently yanked in the opposite direction. The corgis had decided there was something behind us that they really wanted to see.

"One of these days, you're going to dislocate my shoulder by doing that," I scolded the dogs. However, my anger and exasperation flew out the window once I caught sight of the corgis. Both Sherlock and Watson's hackles were raised, and I think both dogs were close to snarling. "What's the matter, guys? Did I miss something? Where's the Boogeyman?"

The dogs started pulling for all they were worth, which had me stumbling forward and trying to wrap the leashes securely around my hand as quickly as I could. I cast a quick glance behind me and saw that Jillian was looking at me with a questioning look on her face. Before I could say anything, I was pulled out the door.

"What are we doing?" I asked the dogs. "Who are we following? Care to give me a clue?"

I was ignored. The dogs pulled as though their lives depended on it, which resulted in me being forced into a fast trot. Now, anyone who knows me will attest to the fact that I'm really not that far out of shape. Sadly, with everything that's happened to us in the last couple of months, I really hadn't had a chance to get back on my exercise equipment. What did that mean? Easy. After a few minutes, I was wheezing like a chain-smoking asthmatic.

"Aw, c-come on, g-guys! This is r-ridiculous! Let me c-catch my breath, huh?"

Whether they took pity on me, or else it was just a freak coincidence, the corgis chose that time to let out a few barks. The group of teens turned to look behind them. They saw the dogs and immediately reversed course. Suddenly, we were surrounded by older kids, who I'd like to add, were polite as could be. Most recognized Sherlock and Watson and asked for permission to pet them. I was about to grant it when I noticed not everyone had wanted to meet the dogs. One kid, a short, slim brown-haired boy wearing a dark hoodie and black jeans, was standing about ten feet away. He was wearing a green camouflage backpack and looked like a deer caught in a pair of headlights. His eyes flicked over to me, traveled down to land on the dogs, and then back at me. I could almost hear the announcer in my head.

On your mark, get set, go!

The kid took off, leaping nimbly over a metal fence. Sherlock and Watson barked excitedly and strained on their leashes, eager to pursue.

"Oh, this is just swell," I wheezed to myself. "Guys? I'm gonna need to find someone with a defib kit after this is over. Go get him!"

I ran as fast as I could. People always assume corgis, having some seriously short legs, wouldn't be able to keep up with someone running at a flat-out sprint. I always argue that corgi owners know otherwise. Those squat little legs are muscular, and are able to keep the dog low to the ground, thus allowing for them to take corners at Mach 2.

Before I knew what was happening, we were barreling through the group of teens, who scattered out of the way like bowling pins. By the time I remembered I should be apologizing for barging through people much smaller than me, we were already well past them. On and on we ran, passing pedestrians, families, dog walkers, and so on. Did we pass one cop? Nope. It was time to call for reinforcements.

"Detective Samuelson," my friend said, as I dialed his number.

"V-Vance? Get over h-here, h-hurry! F-following one of the th-thieves!"

"What? Are you sure?"

"He's r-running from me."

"You take it easy. I don't need you to have a heart attack on my watch. Where are you at?"

"M-main. Just p-passed Wired C-café."

"We're on our way! Don't lose sight of him, old man."

"B-b-b-…"

"Yeah, yeah, I know. Bite me, huh? Just don't lose him!"

We were approaching Third Street when I saw the kid dart into an antique store at the end of the block.

Now, in case you're wondering why so many of the businesses were still open this late in the evening, let me tell you something about the Pacific Northwest. Thanks to daylight savings time, the sun didn't bother setting until much later. Depending on the time of year, sometimes sunset isn't until after 9 p.m. Therefore, business owners—correctly guessing that passing foot traffic would continue as long as the sun was still out—extended their hours to match.

Let Burt be there, let Burt be there, let Burt be there, I chanted silently. That particular antique store was owned and operated by a former Strongman competitor by the name of Burt Johnson. He's helped us out on a few cases before, and I know he wouldn't think twice to help again.

I heard a cry of alarm, and just like that, the kid bolted out the door and darted across the street, narrowly avoiding being struck by a box truck delivery vehicle. Burt Johnson's six-and-a-half-foot frame appeared in his doorway with a look of surprise on his face. He noticed the dogs and me running his way and immediately pointed across the street.

"He's heading back the way he came," he reported. "See him? He's crouching behind the magazine racks in front of the candy store."

Burt then stepped out, into traffic, and held up both hands. Cars on both sides of the street obligingly came to a stop. Throwing my huge friend a thumbs up, the three of us quickly crossed the street and headed toward the confectioner's, which was three or four doors away. The kid saw us coming and resumed running.

Where the hell was Vance? We've been running like crazy, so maybe he didn't know where we presently were?

I risked a glance at my cell as I ran. It was still in my hand, so as I lifted it to call Vance one more time, I saw that the call was still connected! Apparently, I never terminated it.

"M-m-main," I sputtered, as the dogs pulled me through downtown PV. "Passed Second. H-headin' east!"

Whether or not my friend responded, I have no idea. I shoved the phone back in my pocket and focused all energy on not throwing up. Running had never been my strong suit.

A siren sounded from somewhere in the distance. It's about time! Here comes the cavalry! However, I could no longer see the fleeing kid. That meant he had to have snuck into one of the shops. The question was, which one?

The sirens grew louder. My dogs had slowed to a fast walk. Did that mean they could tell our suspect was no longer fleeing? I could only hope they knew where the little punk was hiding.

We had just passed Bella's Baubles, a shop selling souvenirs and jewelry, when both Sherlock and Watson drew up short. They both turned to look at the store.

"What's the matter, guys? Is that where he's hiding?"

I reached for the door just as a family was exiting, holding several bags of whatever trinkets had caught their eye. A husband and wife around my age, followed closely by their daughter, smiled at me as I held open the door. However, once the family passed, I noticed both corgis turned again to stare at the trio.

"Woof!"

Several things happened at the same time. The family turned to see the dogs looking at them, with Watson giving us one of her rare growls. The husband looked at his daughter and cocked his head, as though he was noticing her for the first time. The teenager's eyes widened, and with a cry of alarm, bolted to the left, only to slam into Vance, who caught her before she could fall to the ground. What was going on? Who was this girl and what happened to our suspect?

My eyes were drawn to the girl's mother and father, but seeing the looks of confusion on their faces, it suddenly clicked. Could it be? Was this girl our suspect? It *had* to be. The corgis wouldn't have alerted me to her if he, er, *she* wasn't the one we had been chasing. There was certainly more than meets the eye here.

I heard myself think that thought and it was my turn for my eyes to widen. *More than meets the eye.* Wasn't that the motto for a certain shape-shifting line of popular children's toys? Of course! That's why the Transformers had been classified as a corgi clue. The dogs were trying to tell us important, need-to-know-information about our suspects!

"Don't let her g-go!" I cried out, still wheezing. "She's one of the h-hobbits!"

"Get your hands off me!" the girl snarled as she tried to twist free of Vance's grip. Thankfully, my detective friend was much larger, much stronger, and trained in handling uncooperative suspects

"Cool your jets," Vance snapped back. He looked at me with an incredulous expression on his face. "What's going on, Zack? You think she's one of the thieves we're searching for?"

"Don't you get it?" I asked, as my breath finally started to catch up with me. "I think I've figured it out. The Hobbits of Highton let a girl join their club!"

EIGHT

"This weekend certainly isn't playing out like I thought it'd be," I said, mid-Sunday morning. "I was really looking forward to having fun at the comic con, and seeing what kinds of loot I could find. Now, I'm back in this armor, sounding like a clanking tin can every time I take a step."

"You love that armor and you know it," Jillian argued. "It looks good on you! Besides, you're not scheduled to give it back to your friend Michael until this evening, right?"

I looked at Jillian and grinned. However, since I had the helmet on, she couldn't read my expression.

"A fair point."

"Do you really think the last two members of that gang of thieves will try to come back here?" my wife asked.

"I do. Think about it. All of PV is on high alert. We

heard straight from Captain Ryerson, who confirmed that Medford and the surrounding cities have increased their patrols. And, in case I'm right about this, Vance arranged to have about a dozen undercover cops stationed here. That's on top of the local security the convention center provides, which has also promised us they're increasing their numbers. We're really hoping these guys are as foolish as I think they are."

"I don't think they'll show," Jillian was saying. "Why take the risk?"

"Because they think they're smarter than us," I pointed out. "From their point of view, we're nothing but a bunch of hicks. They have to *prove* they can beat us at our own game."

"And you think they'll come here?" Jillian asked, unable to hide her skepticism.

"I think it's perfect. What are the chances the last two members will return to the scene of the crime? Why wouldn't they just cut their losses and run?"

"Because of their friends," Jillian told me, using a calm voice.

"Precisely. They won't leave them behind. Either they're waiting to pull off a jail break, or else they're working out what they can do to ensure the safe return of their two missing members. Think about it. They're used to pulling off successful heists and escaping scot-free. Now, in a little town in the southern part of the state, and for the first time ever, not one but *two* of their members were captured. No, they're not going to leave here without a fight."

"I wonder what costumes they'll be wearing?" Jillian asked several minutes later. "Based on the elaborate nature of the disguises that were confiscated, I think it's safe to say that these people know how to conceal themselves. They could literally be anybody. Our community might be small compared to the big urban cities these comic cons traditionally use, but we still have stores. This isn't the Stone Age. I'm sure they can find what they need elsewhere."

A notion occurred, one that had me frowning. "What if … what if they *didn't* choose to dress up? What if they went as themselves? How would we know? How do we know those two aren't walking around in broad daylight, dressed as themselves?"

Jillian sighed. "We wouldn't. That is, unless *they*," and she pointed at Sherlock and Watson, who were trotting by my side, "picked up their scent."

"How would that work?" I wondered. "I mean, I don't think they've smelled them before. I guess they could, especially if all four of the gang were here yesterday. We'd be banking on the dogs' short-term memory."

"They found that Phoenix person, didn't they?" Jillian asked.

"Yes, they did. And, speaking about the second hobbit, the girl, I'm pretty sure neither of the dogs smelled his scent before. Er, make that *her* scent. Wow, that was a shocker, wasn't it? I did not think Phoenix was a girl. You can't tell based on the name alone anymore. She almost walked right by us, and I never would have suspected her. After all, it was a fluke coincidence that a husband and wife couple were exiting the store at the same time. All she had to do was tag along behind them—unnoticed—and make her escape, under all of our noses. Well, except for them. Sherlock and Watson weren't faked out at all."

"That's why I'm thinking they'll be able to find them in here," Jillian said. "Provided they are, in fact, here. I don't think it'll matter what they're wearing."

"Speaking of outfits," I began, as I took Jillian's hand in mine and pulled her to a stop. "You never did explain yours. You didn't have to rent that? You actually own it?"

"I told you that I'm a movie fan," Jillian reminded me. "I was invited to a convention in Portland a number of years ago. Michael encouraged me to go, but he fell sick and ... well, you know the rest."

I did, indeed. Jillian's late husband contracted lung cancer from second-hand smoke, and sadly, he passed away less than three months later.

"And you say this is the first time you've worn it?" I wanted to know.

Jillian looked down at the black jump suit she was wearing and gave me a shy smile.

"Out in public, yes. I've tried it on a few times, but I never had the nerve to wear it outside. This is the first time."

For those of you wondering what my gorgeous wife was wearing, let me paint the picture and see if you can guess what character she is supposed to be. First off, she was wearing a black, form-fitting jumpsuit with calf-high black boots. Around her hips were two belts. One was comprised of a series of black pouches, and the second was a black nylon dual gun holster. Each holster was also strapped in place around her thighs, and on her forearms, black bracelets, comprised of what looked like long black tubes, complete with a miniature battery pack discretely tucked away in one of the tubes circling her wrist. At the press of a button, a series of blue LED lights would illuminate the bracelet, simulating an electrical-based weapon.

So, any ideas who she was supposed to be? If you guessed a certain ex-Russian spy, you'd be correct.

To say that my wife looked incredibly fetching in that costume would be a *severe* understatement. Quite frankly, it was a wonder I hadn't collided with anything while we were walking around, since I was constantly shifting my gaze over to her and offering her what I'm sure was a goofy smile. Then again, I kept forgetting that there wasn't any way she could see my face while I had my helmet on.

"Have you found anything you'd like yet?" Jillian asked.

"Oh, I absolutely have."

"That can be bought," Jillian clarified, although if I wasn't mistaken, I do believe my wife was blushing.

"Well …"

"That was a poor choice of words. Let me try again. Have you found anything that you think would be a good match for your theater?"

I looked at the rows and rows of vendor booths and tables.

"Why don't we go take a look? Sherlock, Watson? Care to go exploring?"

The dogs, I'm sure, viewed this as just another outing. They eagerly looked up at each person we passed, hoping beyond hope that they might be careless with a crumb of food, or have a doggie biscuit. Time and time again, they'd receive a pat on the head, or a friendly scratch behind their ears, and then move off. It had happened so frequently that I was now waiting for the exasperated snort after each greeting.

"Not everyone is Vance, pal," I told the corgis. "All us bipeds don't typically carry around a never-ending bag of doggie treats. You need to remember that, 'kay?"

"Hey, you! Zack!"

Jillian and I turned at the sound of someone calling my name. A man I didn't recognize, standing nearly twenty feet away, was motioning for me to come over.

"Who's that?" Jillian asked.

"Beats me. Let's see what he wants."

The crowds parted around us, and we overheard quite a few people talking about the costumes we were wearing. Who are we kidding? With Jillian looking like that, there was no way anyone was looking in my direction. And do you know what? I was fine with it.

"Do I know you?" I asked, as I stepped in front of the stranger.

"No, sorry. I don't know you, either." The stranger pointed behind him. "She asked me to flag you down. Lucky dog."

Sherlock and Watson perked up.

"I wasn't talking about you guys," the man added.

He nodded once at me and moved off. As soon as he did, we discovered we were at a small group of tables that had attracted quite a following. Jennifer Blanc-Biehn was there, chatting with a woman behind the table who I knew I recognized from somewhere, but couldn't place it. Jennifer waved me over, but once she saw Jillian, her face lit up in a dazzling smile.

"Ooo, I love your costume, Jillian! Where did you get it?"

"Honestly? I don't remember. I've had it a number of years now. I was just telling Zachary that I normally don't wear this out in public."

"You should, girl. It looks fantastic on you! Don't you agree, Zack?"

I nodded. "You'd better believe it. Where's Michael?"

"He and Dash are just around the corner. We saw you walk by from a distance. He wanted to talk to you."

"Lead the way, m'lady."

We followed Jennifer through one crowd only to arrive at a second. Naturally, Michael had once again attracted a significant following. When we arrived, he was in the midst of telling a group of listeners about some excursion he took to the rural parts of Arizona, and nearly dying while looking for a famous cowboy's grave located at the remains of some historical cabin. Their son, Dashiel, had dozed off in a chair behind them.

"There they are. How are my favorite amateur detectives?"

I laughed and pointed at the dogs. "I know you're not talking about me. We're good. How are you guys doing?"

Michael turned to the next person in line, greeted them, and signed a new-in-box action figure of himself from one of the many movies he's been in.

"Living the life, brother. Listen, I was wondering if you had any updates about the … oh, hello there. Aren't you dashing in that getup?"

A ten-year-old boy was standing at the front of the line, holding a complicated toy gun. The child kept looking at his father, who nodded his head and encouraged him to continue.

"Would you like me to sign that?" Michael asked, looking at the father for confirmation. When the dad nodded, Michael took the gun which, oddly enough, was a dart gun recreation of the weapon that was stolen yesterday, and signed his name across the barrel. "There you go, all right? Make sure to keep those aliens at bay, you got it?"

The father thanked him and steered his son off.

"I think I'm in the wrong profession," I said, chuckling.

"You're really not," Jillian told me. "You're paid to do the same things for your publisher."

She had me there.

"You were looking for an update?" I asked.

Michael nodded. "If you've got one."

I relayed everything that had happened in the last twenty-four hours, culminating with the capture of the second hobbit. Michael returned to signing autographs and posing for pictures as I recounted our exploits.

"He's still listening to us, right?" I asked Jennifer.

"Of course. That man is a multi-tasker."

Once I had finished, Michael seemed more impressed with the dogs than he had before.

"You're a writer, right? You ought to think about putting those dogs down on paper. We know a lot of people in Hollywood. I think they'd be great on a set."

"TV movies," Jennifer decided. "I remember reading about your dogs solving some Irish crime. People would *love* to watch a story like that unfold on television."

"I'll keep that in mind," I said, grinning. "Listen, I wanted to apologize about canceling dinner plans with you guys last night. I'm really hoping we can reschedule. Maybe tonight? If you're free?"

Michael looked at Jennifer, who eagerly nodded.

"You name the time and place, and we'll be there," Michael promised.

I automatically looked at Jillian. "Where should we go?"

"Do you like Mexican? Or, if you prefer something more American, there's this fantastic place with the largest grill I've ever seen."

"Great ribs, and steaks …" I began.

"That sounds good," Michael decided.

"… and sausages, and brisket, and …"

"It's safe to say Zack isn't a vegetarian?" Jennifer asked.

My wife nodded. "Far from it."

"… and smoked pork, and barbecued chicken, and …"

Jillian placed a hand over my mouth. "You win, dear. Marauder's Grill it is. Let me check to see when they close. Oh, we're good. They won't close until 11 p.m. tonight."

"Restaurants stay open that late around here?" Michael asked, impressed.

"They do if they have bars attached to them," I said, nodding.

We bade our celebrity friends adieu, and promised to let them know of any new developments.

"We haven't had any hits," I said, nearly ten minutes later, as we breezed by the various items for sale by the many vendors. "I'm starting to think that maybe this wasn't such a good idea after all."

"You just have to give it time," Jillian was saying. She was flipping through a box of vinyl records. "I'm sure you'll find something sooner or later."

"We're talking about our halfling friends, right?"

My wife looked up and giggled. "Oh, I thought you were talking about finding something to display in your theater."

"We'll get to that. But first, do you think we're wasting our time here? After all, I don't feel like we're any closer to finding that gun than we were when we first learned it had been stolen."

"You have always told me to have faith in the dogs,"

Jillian reminded me. "This case isn't over, and there are still two members of the hobbit gang to locate. They're here. Somewhere."

"How can you be so certain?"

"Because of their inferiority complex. They think they're smarter than everyone else. How can they prove that? By pulling off even more daring feats. I'm certain they're not only here, but that they're planning on pulling something else off, just to let us know that they can."

"How are we going to find them?" I asked.

Jillian held out a hand, indicating the row of booths.

"By doing what we're doing now: mingling. We're calmly searching for something to buy. We're being seen in the process. Let's keep doing what we're doing and see what happens."

"Shopping? You're saying that the best thing for us to be doing right now is shopping?"

Jillian burst out laughing. "I know, I know. It doesn't sound very scientific, but I truly believe we're on the right path. Now, let's get going, shall we? What about these? This nice man has a lovely selection of superhero figurines. Would you like one of these? Do you have a favorite?"

I was trying very hard not to keep looking over my shoulder. I could almost *feel* the many sets of eyes on me, and part of me was wondering if any of them belonged to our group of nerds. Er, hobbits. Great, now Vance had me slandering them.

"Not really. Superheroes aren't really my thing. If you spot something from *Star Wars*, especially vehicles, then you'll know you're on the right track."

"*Star Wars*. Got it."

We found a huge selection of rolled up movie posters

at the next booth. Looking at the dozens and dozens of boxes holding long tubes of paper, much like department stores displaying wrapping paper during the holiday season, I sidled close to the proprietor.

"Got anything from *Star Wars*?"

The vendor, a sixty-something portly fellow wearing a button-down, short-sleeve shirt and a pair of khakis, scratched his several days growth of stubble.

"Well, let me think."

Suddenly, a notion occurred. Why hadn't I thought of it before?

"Scratch that. What about *Aliens*? Or the original *Terminator*?"

The vendor was nodding. "I see where you're going with this. I know Michael Biehn is currently here. Let me see what I have."

While he searched, I joined Jillian at her box and we started rummaging through the rolled tubes. Thankfully, the vendor had written the movie name on the side. Jillian slid a tube out and held it up, like she had just pulled Excalibur from its stone.

"Here we go. This is the one you need to buy."

"Well, color me intrigued. Which one is it?"

"*The Abyss*."

I turned to look in the direction we had just come. "Think I could get Michael to sign it? After all, he makes a great villain."

"Michael wasn't the villain in that movie," Jillian argued. "He was just misunderstood. He wasn't acting normally, he was suffering from the shakes, and … what?"

"I'm so proud of you," I said, as I pulled her in for a hug. "Did you know all of that on your own, or was that something you picked up from me?"

"I've heard you talk about it on many occasions," Jillian admitted. "I know it's one of your favorite movies."

I took the tube. "Consider it sold. Excuse me? I'd like to buy this one."

"Did you find the *Terminator*?" the vendor asked. He also held up a tube. "I did find a poster for the other movie you wanted."

"*Aliens*? I'll take that, too. Thanks."

With my purchases in hand, and resisting the temptation to toss a rolled poster to Jillian and have our own sword fight right there in the middle of the convention, we returned to examining the many offerings waiting to be purchased.

I didn't think I was going to find anything else I wanted. They had a wide selection of items, don't get me wrong. I think there was something for everyone. I just felt like, I don't know, the *caliber* of the items wasn't quite up to my liking. That is, until we stepped around the corner and I was suddenly facing a booth that had a selection of swords and weapons proudly displayed.

"Hoo boy," Jillian sighed, giving me a smile. "Here we go."

"I think I'm in heaven," I moaned. I pointed at a replica of Sting, Bilbo's dagger. "Well, let's start there, shall we?"

Four swords, two dirks, and one phurba later, and after running the load out to the car, we got our first indication that our theories about the hobbits were correct. And, for the record, I was still holding my two posters. After all, I needed them signed before they could be displayed, didn't I?

"Woof."

I pulled my helmet off and looked down at my tri-colored boy.

"What is it? Do you smell something?"

Sherlock whined once and looked left, which was farther away from the front entrance.

"One of the other two must be here," Jillian whispered.

I gave the dogs some extra slack in their leashes.

"Go on, guys. Lead the way. Let's see if we can get number three, huh?"

The dogs made a complete circuit of the convention grounds, before leading us back inside. There we must've passed every single booth and table. Thankfully, we were ignored, mostly because most people weren't looking at the floor and didn't notice the dogs. No one will, as long as I'm walking next to Jillian. Wearing her black skin-tight outfit, with her hair styled in a tight braid, would make anyone look twice.

I saw that we were approaching Michael's table once more. Like before, he still had a long line of admirers who were waiting to meet him and his wife. He looked up at me as I approached and before either of us could say anything, I pointed at my posters and then at him. My new friend nodded and tapped the table, indicating I should leave the posters there. That's when I saw it.

Prominently displayed on the counter, sitting less than two feet away from Michael, was a book. In fact, it was a cookbook, and one didn't need to be a master detective to figure out where the book was purchased. I felt the blood drain from my face.

I tapped Jillian on the shoulder.

"Look, but don't touch. What book is sitting on the table over there?"

"Where? Next to Michael? Oh, I see it. It looks like … well, it looks like something I would sell, doesn't it?"

"They were there," I whispered, to myself.

Jillian pulled me around so that I was facing her. She tapped my helmet, indicating she wanted me to take it off.

"What did you say?"

"Earlier, when we caught Phoenix. He was coming out of …"

"She," Jillian interrupted.

"Whatever. She was coming out of Cookbook Nook. That book? They were clearly there, and they obviously know you're connected to me. I don't like this one bit."

"What's this?" I suddenly heard Michael say.

I'm ashamed to say I snatched up one of the rolled-up posters laying nearby and smacked Michael's hand with it. I don't know who was more surprised, him or me.

"Sorry. That book? By any chance, did you see who placed it there?"

Michael shrugged. "Not really. I had my attention focused elsewhere. Jen, did you see who put this here?"

Jennifer stared at the book and shook her head. "I didn't. I was helping Dashiel get his tablet connected to the Wi-fi here. For some reason, he was kicked off."

I saw a box of tissues nearby, and using one, I gently opened the cookbook. There, inside the front cover, was a folded piece of paper. Taking it, I unfolded it on the table and we all read the printed message.

VIOLATION AGAINST THE HOBBITS OF HIGHTON. CRIMES COMMITTED ARE SEVERE. UNLESS STEPS ARE TAKEN, RETALIATION WILL COME.

"What is that supposed to mean?" Jennifer asked, growing nervous.

I sighed. "They want their people back."

That night, when the four of us met for dinner at what could only be called a carnivore's ultimate dream, locally known as the Marauder's Grill, we all recapped how our day went.

"I signed your posters for you," Michael was saying. "There's an *Aliens* reunion coming up that I've been invited to. Say the word, and I'll take your poster along and have everyone sign it for you."

My eyes shot open. "Are you kidding me? I'd love that! Thanks!"

"Anytime, brother. Now, would you care to fill us in on why that cookbook was dropped off at my table? I damn near signed the flippin' thing before Jen stopped me."

"You know about the Hobbits, right?"

Michael nodded. "It's what the thieves call themselves."

"Right. We've caught two. That's why we were there. We had this crazy notion that the remaining two members might be hiding at the convention. That's why we went back. By the way, thanks again for the use of the armor. I can't even begin to wonder how much that thing costs."

"I promised to return it in good condition," Michael told me. "He didn't tell me either. The only thing he said was that it was one of four suits used on the show. One of the stuntmen who plays the main character is about your size."

I'm sure my jaw hit the floor. "I was wearing a screen-used suit of armor? I did not know that. Probably good that I didn't. Anyway, that cookbook was purchased in

Jillian's store. The remaining two members were letting us know that, if they wanted to, they could get their greasy hooks on my wife."

"I don't like that at all," Jennifer said.

"Neither do I," Michael added. "What can we do?"

The waitress arrived at our table and took our drink order. She hesitated as she looked at Michael, but then walked away.

"You've already done more than enough," I told them. "This is our case. We're going to get it solved for you. I can't have you guys having a negative experience in Oregon, especially in our neck of the woods."

"Excuse me?" a woman's voice asked.

We all turned to see that the waitress had returned. This time, she was accompanied by two other people. One was wearing a white apron, and another had on a long-sleeve business shirt and black slacks.

"By any chance, are you Michael Biehn?" the man in the white apron asked.

Michael grinned. He looked at the small group and nodded.

"I don't usually say this for people, but I will for you. *Come with me if you want to live.*"

The person wearing the white shirt and black slacks extended a hand.

"Percy Adamson. I'm the general manager here. It's a pleasure to meet you, Mr. Biehn. We are thrilled you and your guests have chosen to dine with us tonight. We ... Jillian? I'm so sorry, Mrs. Anderson. I didn't see you there. You're acquainted with Mr. Biehn? Well, of course you are. Why wouldn't you be?"

"This happens to me all the time," I whispered to

Michael, but loud enough that everyone could hear it. "It probably means she owns this place."

My wife swatted my arm. "Hello, Percy. It's good to see you. How is Erin?"

"She's doing well, Mrs. Anderson, thank you for asking. I won't take up any more of your time. Mr. Biehn, it was a pleasure. Mrs. Anderson, if there's anything you or your guests need, please let us know."

For the next hour and a half, the four of us sat and talked as though we had known each other our entire lives. Michael regaled us with a few of his interactions with some incredibly famous people. I provided the comic relief by telling stories about my early attempts at being a writer. Back then, I went to great lengths to hide behind my pseudonym and was embarrassed to tell anyone what profession I had chosen.

We heard all about how Michael and Jennifer had met, the different movies they were in together, and that the work *behind* the camera was much more intense than anything happening in front. I was thrilled when Michael launched into his experiences during the filming of *The Abyss* and *Aliens*, two of my favorites. I heard all about the trials and tribulations of *Tombstone*, and his inspiration to set the record straight regarding common misconceptions about certain things history has gotten wrong. We heard about a good friend of his that was cheated out of a promising acting part in what turned out to be a very iconic war movie. I also discovered he had been good friends with the late Bill Paxton, and starred in five movies together.

Trust me when I say that it was a movie fan's ultimate night. But, all good things inevitably come to an end. In my case, it happened when my cell rang. And, of course, it could only be Vance.

"I probably should take this," I apologized, standing up. "Vance? Hold on a second…"

Once I was outside, and pacing in the parking lot, I heard news that shocked me to my core: somehow and no one knew how, one of the hobbits had escaped.

NINE

"This is *not* how I thought this weekend was going to go," I said, nearly thirty minutes later as I strolled back through the Pomme Valley police department's front doors. My detective friend was waiting. "How many times can one person possibly visit the police station in a span of two days? This is getting insane. I'm tired, the dogs are tired, and Jillian? I sent her home in my car. So, do we have any idea how he got away?"

"Trust me, we're going through our security footage," Vance assured me. "They *had* to have help. I want to know who it was, and what avenue they used to make their escape."

"Who escaped?" I wanted to know. "Alex or Phoenix?"

"Alex."

I followed Vance as we rounded the front counter and headed for the interior of the station. To say that it was a hive of activity was an understatement. Based on the frantic activity of everyone present, I could easily believe that a full-blown riot was happening, only I knew that wasn't the case.

"Right under our own flippin' noses!" I heard an angry voice exclaim. I didn't need to wonder who that could be. And, for the record, that wasn't the word he used. Let's leave it at that. Captain Nelson's gruff voice was recognizable almost anywhere. Like us, he was apparently experiencing a long day, too. "I want the cells dusted. I want every available eye trained on our security footage. Someone came in here. Someone managed to get our perp's cell open and then waltz out of here in broad daylight. "Samuelson, tell me you found that damn gun. Has Anderson ... Speak of the devil. You've got good news for me?"

I shook my head. "I'm sorry, Sir. Not yet. We are making progress, but it's happening much too slowly for my liking."

"Keep at it. Inform me the moment anything happens, you got that?"

"Absolutely, Sir."

"Dietrich, Markus, back to that blasted comic book show."

"Convention," someone corrected, using a quiet voice. "It's over for tonight. They'll be back at it tomorrow."

"For a half-day," I added.

"Fine," the captain grumped. "See to it you're there the moment it opens tomorrow. Where's Pettit?"

"We received a tip that a van full of college-age kids

were getting too rough at Red Barn Tavern, but it turned out to be a false alarm," Julie reported. "I'm sorry, Captain. I know the recovery of this suspect is our priority, but we cannot ignore the calls that do come in."

"No, you're right, Jules," Captain Nelson said. His frown remained in place. "I want to know the instant anyone hears anything, is that understood?"

A chorus of *yes sirs* echoed around the room. The captain then turned to look pointedly at the dogs before lifting his gaze to settle it on me. I nodded once. He nodded back and stalked out of the room.

"Julie, shouldn't you be gone by now?" I asked.

"I warned Harrison that this could be a long weekend," Julie told me. "We were told that, until this case is wrapped up, plan on getting some overtime."

"Where do we go from here?" I asked Vance, who immediately pointed at the dogs.

"Let's take them to Alex's cell. Maybe they can pinpoint something worth investigating? Maybe they'll sense something is off? Right now, I'd take a hunch."

"Sherlock? Watson? You heard him. Let's go."

Vance turned on his heel and proceeded through the nearest doorway, which was the corridor that would take us to the large holding pen, and six smaller individual cells. We stopped at the second cell, which I thought looked no different than the others.

"How the blazes did he get out of this?" I wondered aloud, as I looked at the thick metal bars and the heavy-duty locking mechanism on the door. "There's no way!"

"We're looking into it," Vance assured me. "He couldn't have gotten far. I'll personally throw away the key once he's back in there."

I snorted with laughter. Vance gave me a look that said *try me* before he pulled out a ring of keys and unlocked Alex's former cell. Stepping aside, I let Sherlock and Watson enter first. Both dogs sniffed along the bottom of the cot before moving to the stainless-steel toilet in the corner. They each snorted—in stereo—before turning to look up at me.

"What did you expect it to smell like, roses?"

Sherlock regarded me for a few moments before he brushed by me, intent on leaving the cell.

"Looks like there's nothing in here worth investigating," I decided. "Guys? Take the lead. Is there something in here you need to show us?"

Sherlock and Watson tugged on their leashes. That could only be encouraging, to say the least. The dogs led us down the hall, past the last cell, before stopping at a locked door. Curious, I looked back at Vance, ready to ask if he knew what was behind door number one.

"It's just a janitor closet. There's nothing to see in there."

Both corgis immediately sat. Smiling profusely, I looked back at my friend and hooked a thumb at the dogs. "Methinks they doth have a difference of opinion, m'lord."

"Jerk. Fine, I think I've got a key here for that."

The door was unlocked and held open. Sherlock and Watson strutted through, as though they owned the place. Vance was right. There was nothing in there but custodial supplies: mops, buckets, spray bottles, yellow folding caution signs, and various jugs of chemicals.

"See? What would you …?"

Sherlock turned on his heel and exited the closet just as quickly as he had entered. Watson followed close behind.

"Now where are we going?" Vance wanted to know.

"Beats me. The only worthwhile thing I do for them is fill their bowls with food."

The dogs led us through a few more corridors before coming to a stop at another locked door.

"Another janitor's closet," Vance said, as he read the *Custodial* placard set into the door. After a few attempts, he unlocked the door and held it open for the dogs. "Do you two see anything in here that you like?"

Sherlock and Watson lost interest the moment the door was opened.

"I do believe this might be relevant," I said, using my best fake British accent I could come up with. "Cheerio, I'm going to take a photograph."

"What did you put in your soda today? A shot of extra-strength doofus?"

I chuckled. "Well, if you'd stop leaving it out in the open and just finish it off when you …"

"Don't go there," Vance mock-warned, cutting me off. Shaking his head, he looked down at the dogs, who were now anxious to move on. "What do we do? Follow them?"

I shrugged and was about to suggest we call it a day, when I caught sight of the blinking red light above the security camera covering the hallway. Turning, I saw two more cameras covering the junction of a hallway running perpendicular to the one we were in.

"You guys already have people reviewing the security footage," I began, "but have you told them to look for janitors?"

"No. Why would we? Oh. The janitor closets? Is that their way of telling us to check into the cleaning crew?"

"You know the dogs almost as well as I do," I reminded

my friend. "It's just a suggestion."

Vance nodded and pointed at the corridor on our right. "Come on. Let's spread the word. Who can access the offline server for security footage? Anyone here have the credentials to do it?"

"I do," Officer Jones announced. "I can get to the server from any computer, provided I log into our VPN first. To do that, we would need to …"

"I don't need to know the specifics," Captain Nelson's voice snapped, as he seemingly appeared out of thin air. "A yes or no will do."

"What am I looking for? A janitor? I see them all the time. What's so special about this one?"

"Because the cleaning crew doesn't get here until after eight, unless requested," the captain barked. "So, have we?"

"Er, have we *what*?" Jones asked.

"Requested a cleaning crew to come in early," Vance said. My detective friend was already frowning. "Judging by the silence, I'm guessing that's a *no*."

The captain snapped his fingers and pointed at the nearest computer. Jones was already busy typing away on his keyboard.

"Start searching. Look for anyone who looks like a janitor. I want to know when they were seen last And, based on the source of the tip, I'm guessing I'm not gonna like the answer."

"Who's the source?" Officer Jones asked.

Standing behind the captain, I shook my head no and then pointed at the dogs. Jones' face sobered and he immediately started tapping like crazy on his computer. Captain Nelson looked up and saw that most everyone in the large room was now staring at him.

"What are y'all starin' at? Get your butts back to work! I swear, it's like I'm talkin' to a brick wall. A janitor, people. You're lookin' for a janitor."

"One that would have arrived before five," I added.

The captain nodded. "Precisely. I want to know when they …"

"Got one!" someone exclaimed.

We all hurried to the officer's desk. There, visible on the monitor, was a sharp, clear image of a single figure pushing a mop bucket along the hallway, mopping the floor as they went.

"What time is this?" Vance wanted to know.

"Just after seven. Seven-fifteen, to be precise."

Captain Nelson was silent as he watched the custodian slowly work their way down the hall.

"Have we verified with the cleaning crew that no one was here at that time?"

We heard a phone's cradle being replaced on its base.

"I just did," Officer Jones reported. "It wasn't them."

"That's our guy," Vance said, seething with anger. "Follow him, Reynolds. Let's see where he goes, and whether or not we can get a shot of his face."

As we all huddled around the desk, staring at the footage in silence, one thing became abundantly clear: whoever that person was, they knew *exactly* where the cameras were located. A spin here, a subtle turn of the head there, and just now, the figure hunched over and remained that way until passing several windows. Every time the janitor's face came close to being exposed, he would twist, or bob and weave, or whatever he could do to keep it hidden from sight.

"He knows," Captain Nelson said, as if reading our

thoughts. "He knows where our cameras are, and how much they can cover. Keep it rolling, Reynolds. Let's see if we're right, and this guy finds a way to break his buddy out. Where's he at now?"

"Passing the holding tank," Vance reported. "Look at this. No one is even bothering to look at him! It's like he's ... he's ..."

"... invisible," I finished. "I've used a few janitors as characters in my novels. Vance is right. They're one of the few professions who can move around with absolute stealth. Why? It's because no one pays attention to them."

"Not anymore," the captain grumbled. "There, look. He's mopping the floor in front of the cells. Which one held the Alex kid?"

"Number two," Jones answered, after consulting a printed handout next to his computer. "It'll be the second cell from the left."

"Watch him closely," Vance instructed. "We ... well, that wasn't obvious at all, was it?"

We had all just watched the janitor wander close to the cells and very deliberately pull something loose from under his uniform to shove it through the cell bars.

"What was that?" I asked. "Can anyone tell?"

"Jonesy, can you zoom in on that upper left quadrant?" Vance asked.

A blinking blue box appeared on the screen. Officer Jones dragged it to the top left corner of the video, resized it to include only the areas they wanted to observe, and hit the enter key. The video jumped back five seconds and the highlighted area immediately expanded to fill the screen. Play was pressed, and the video commenced running once more.

Mesmerized, we all watched the janitor shove a small bundle through the bars without breaking stride. Alex, stretched out on his cot, didn't move until the custodian had wandered off. Working quickly, our suspect unrolled the bundle, revealing a set of clothes. Moments later, he was dressed in an identical janitorial uniform. A baseball cap with a bent bill appeared, and was placed on his head.

"Oh, son of a biscuit," I moaned. "That's how he walked out of here. He pretended to be one of the janitors."

"And no one looked twice," Vance said, scowling.

I felt a couple of gentle tugs on the leashes and looked down. Sherlock and Watson were now stretched out on the floor, moments away from falling asleep. I couldn't fault them. They had to be tired. After all, they alerted us to the janitors, and with their help, we pinpointed how Alex escaped. Only ...

"He's still in his cell," I pointed out. "How does he get out?"

In the video, we watched the small figure, now dressed in a janitor's uniform, approach his cell door. He pulled something from his pocket, reached through the bars, and began fiddling with the lock. "He's trying to pick it, isn't he?"

"Those locks are extremely difficult to pick," Vance said. "It's not like they are standard tumbler locks. You'd have to be an expert at ..."

The cell door opened.

"You were saying, Detective?" the captain asked, folding his arms across his chest.

"That took less than ten seconds," I observed. Then, I found everyone staring at me. "Hey, you saw the same thing I did. That clearly isn't the first time Alex has picked a lock. He knew what he was doing."

"Follow him," Captain Nelson ordered. "Where does he go from here?"

Our group fell silent as we tracked the fake janitor through various frames until he, quite confidently, strolled past Julie at the front desk. He stopped long enough to wave a hand in greeting as he exited the front door.

No one said a word. We sat there, as the footage played, in complete silence. Then, according to the time-stamp on the video, five minutes later, the first guy, still wearing his janitor get-up, strolled by and also waved at Julie. My friend's wife beamed a smile and waved back.

"Get Jules," Captain Nelson ordered.

"Now, I don't think she had any idea who those people were," Vance began. "We can't ..."

"I want to know if she saw either of their faces," Captain Nelson explained. "I'm not going to criticize her, Samuelson. Take it down a notch."

A few moments later, Julie Watt joined us.

"Hey, Captain. What's going on?"

"Rewind the footage and then play it back," Captain Nelson ordered. "Jules? Watch the screen. There. Do you recognize either of these two?"

Julie fell silent as she watched the footage of herself play on the computer monitor. She smiled and nodded after the second janitor pushed his way through the front door.

"The janitors? Sure, I remember them. Friendly fellows. What did you want to know about them?"

"Did you see either of their faces?" Vance asked. I noticed his notebook was in his hand and a pen was ready.

"Hmm, let me think. I don't really recall seeing their

faces. They each told me to have a good day and I didn't think anything else of it. Why do you ask? Who are they?"

"The first one to go out the door is our primary suspect," Vance said, eliciting a gasp of shock from Julie, "and the second was the one who essentially broke him out of jail."

"That's why you wanted to know if I saw their faces," Julies said, shaken. "Oh, I wish I had been paying more attention. I want to help catch these guys."

"Maybe you can," I said. The room fell silent again as all eyes turned my way. "Jules, you said that they told you to have a nice day. Did I hear that right?"

Julie nodded. "That's right. Why?"

"What do you remember about their voices?" I asked. "Deep? Gruff? Did it sound like they were disguising them?"

"Neither of them were that deep," Julie recalled.

"Age?" Vance pressed.

"Umm, college-age?"

Vance jotted the note down. He looked around the room, waiting to see if anyone could think of anything else to ask.

"Build?" I asked.

Vance nodded. "And Zack comes up with a good one. Jules? How would you describe them?"

"Slender," Julie decided.

"Athletic?" Vance asked.

Julie took a few moments to think about her response before she shook her head.

"No, I'd still go with slender."

"Slender it is," Vance said, adding that detail to his notes.

"I do remember thinking it was strange seeing a janitor here before eight. After all, they typically will wait until everyone has gone home for the day."

"We are going to institute some type of training where we all learn to be more observant," the captain muttered. "Samuelson? This is your case. How do you want to proceed?"

My detective friend sighed and rested a hip on a nearby desk. "We lock this town down. We watch all exits. We ... Zack? Put your hand down. We're not in school."

"What is it, Anderson?" the captain asked.

"Phoenix. Where is she?"

Alarmed, Vance looked at Captain Nelson. "Where *is* she? She should've been back by now."

We all watched the chief of police pick up a nearby desk phone and dial a number.

"Captain Ryerson, please. Yeah, I'll hold, just don't keep me waiting too long. What's that? This is Captain Nelson, in PV. Yes, thank you. Ryerson, get some eyes on your guest. Our guy just escaped. One of his friends, disguised as a janitor, just broke him out. She ... what do you mean she's not there? How long ago did you send her back? Look, pal, I don't mean to step on any toes here, but did you not think to check whether or not they made it here?"

"This doesn't sound good," I whispered to Vance, who only nodded.

It was at this exact moment that four more people joined our group, only no one noticed. The dogs did, thank goodness. Sherlock waggled his stump of a tail and immediately dropped to the ground to roll onto his back.

Feeling the tension in his leash, I turned to see what

Sherlock was doing and came to face to face with Detective Amanda Cartez, from the MPD, along with two officers I didn't know, each on the arm of one sullen-looking prisoner.

"There's a friendly face I'm damn glad to see," I said, raising my voice.

There was a collective gasp of surprise. Dozens of questions erupted, all at the same time.

"Time out," Detective Cartez called, holding up her hands. "What's going on here? What'd we miss?"

I pointed at Phoenix, who had suddenly started smiling. "You know, don't you? Well, I'm personally looking forward to wiping that smirk off your face. Amanda, our first suspect managed to escape, thanks to the assistance from one of their friends."

"You'll never see him again," Phoenix chortled. "I figure it'll only be a matter of time before I join them."

"Why aren't you with them now?" I said, confused. "I would've thought they would have snatched you, too."

Phoenix's smile quickly melted into a frown. Captain Nelson pushed his way through the crowd and placed himself before Detective Cartez.

"Anderson brings up a good point. Strategically speaking, it would've been a fantastic time to pull off a jail break. Cartez, you didn't have backup, and you were on your way to here, from there. Why didn't they try it?"

Amanda shrugged. "Well, it might have something to do with a detour we had to make."

"Detour?" Vance said, interested. "What detour?"

"There was an accident on Highway 238. A semi-truck flipped over, making one helluva mess. We had to take the scenic route to get here."

I looked at Vance and grinned. "That's why they didn't get her. They were probably waiting to ambush them, only they didn't get the chance."

Vance slapped a hand on Phoenix's back. "Oh, that's gotta sting, huh? All that planning for naught. Well, don't worry. We'll get you reunited with your buddies soon enough."

"Fat chance, cop."

"Take her to Interrogation Room Two," Captain Nelson ordered. "Better make yourself comfy," he told the young thief, as she was led away. "We're gonna talk about what happened earlier today, you get me?"

"I'll make a fresh pot of coffee," Julie decided.

"Need me for anything else?" I asked, as Vance started to follow the captain toward the interrogation room.

"Nah, you should probably take off. Save yourself. If you hang around here, you're liable to get corralled into sitting in the observation room. Personally, I don't think the captain is gonna let this go until he gets Phoenix to talk."

"She doesn't strike me as the type of person who is easily intimidated."

"And that's why I'm urging you to run for the hills. Escape while you can, pal."

Nodding, the dogs and I headed for the door. Once more, my Jeep was pointed toward home, only something told me I should call my wife first. It's a good thing I did. Jillian wasn't home, but back at Cookbook Nook.

"What in the world are you doing in here so late?" I asked, as I was let in through the locked door. "What is it now, nearly eleven?"

"I couldn't sleep," Jillian said. "I knew you were still

awake, and so were the dogs. I thought I could come here and find something to do, only once I sat down, I couldn't bring myself to get back up. Sounds like you had all kinds of fun at the station."

I took a chair next to hers in the lounge. "That and then some. Alex may have escaped, but at least we know how it was done."

We heard a *woof*.

"Yes, Sherlock, I know it was you. I'm sure Jillian knows it, too."

"I do," Jillian confirmed. "So, what's the plan now? What does Vance want to do?"

"I'm starting to think we might have met our match with these punk kids. They've clearly done their homework. They knew all about the station, where the cameras were, and how to avoid showing their faces. We have no idea who—or what—the person who broke Alex out of his cell looks like." I told Jillian all about how we suspected they also wanted to break the other one out, but thanks to an unexpected detour during the prisoner transport, it had been thwarted. "For all I know, we could be barking up the wrong tree." Both dogs perked up. "Sorry, guys. Bad analogy. What do you think? I'm starting to realize that most of our theories about this gang of thieves are all pure conjecture. We don't have a shred of evidence."

"What about corgi clues?"

"Just as unhelpful as ever. Monopoly? Transformers? And fried chicken? Come on. How are we supposed to figure that out?"

Jillian laid a reassuring hand over my own. "Just like we always do—with help. Lots and lots of help."

"You're suggesting we get the gang together and review the clues?"

"You don't have much more time," my wife pointed out. "The convention wraps up by mid-day tomorrow. Something tells me that, once the convention is over and done, the chances of finding Michael Biehn's missing prop gun will become practically non-existent."

"You're right," I said, nodding. "I personally think the rest of the gang is going to retrieve that gun, wherever it's hiding, and high-tail it out of here. The one plus here is that I'm pretty sure they're not going to want to leave their friend behind."

"And now that we know they'll undoubtedly try to spring their companion?" Jillian asked. "What then?"

"We sit and wait, I guess."

Sherlock gave himself a vigorous shaking, causing his collar to jingle like crazy. Something had just gotten his attention.

"Oh, come on," I complained. "You're gonna make me get up, aren't you? Can't you see we're having a moment?" I heard Jillian giggle softly. Sherlock, however, was unmoved. He was on his feet and looking off to the left.

"What are they doing?" Jillian asked.

"I'm not sure. They're acting like they want to check out the store."

"Well, let them."

I let the leashes drop. "All right, guys. Hit me with your best shot. Let's see what you've got."

For the most part, the corgis stuck together. They moved from rack to rack, sniffing and craning their necks to look at the many books piled high above them. For the first time ever, I got the distinct impression that they were looking for something. Typically, they'd just pull me over to whatever I was supposed to notice. This time, I think they were trying to help me out, only I had no idea how.

Ten minutes later, after having moved from one rack to the other, we approached the *Specialty Baking* rack and here the dogs paused.

"You're kidding. You guys want to bake a cake?" I caught sight of the types of books displayed on the shelves. "Oh, this gets even better. You want to decorate a cake? You're officially off your rocker. And I thought I was tired."

The dogs snorted. Unfortunately for me, I recognized the nature of that snort. It said I had just been demoted to *Ungainly Biped* and that, if I wanted to redeem myself in their eyes, then I'd have to figure out what I was looking for, *fast*.

"There is nothing here but books on how to decorate a cake! How am I supposed to know what I'm looking for?" A mental picture flashed before my eyes. In it, I was watching the director of a world-famous aquarium search through a large crate of life jackets, one by one. Sighing, I reached for the first book on the top shelf. "Oh, this had better be good, guys. Fine. Is it this one? Or this one? What about this?"

On and on this went, with me pulling a book from the shelf and presenting it to the dogs. The corgis, for their part, stared at me with a rather condescending look on their canine features. Ever been given a patronizing look by a dog? That's what I was getting right now.

On the third shelf from the bottom, I struck gold. I held up a book, twisted to show it to the dogs, and was ready to replace it when I heard something that was music to my ears.

"Awwooowooo!"

It was Sherlock. Both dogs were now staring at the book I was holding. I held it up high, then low, and then slowly moved it from left and right. The corgis tracked it as though I was holding a plate of freshly grilled meat. Surprised, I glanced at the title and sighed. More decorating, obviously, but this one specifically taught the techniques used when working with something called fondant.

I took the book back to the lounge and settled down to see if I could determine what had caught the dogs' attention. Then again, seeing how they acted like they didn't know what they were looking for, it made me wonder if I would even recognize the clue when I saw it.

"How to work with fondant," I read, flipping the book open. "Chapter one. This is some really dull reading, guys. I hope you know what you're doing." Figuring I should be looking for a picture of some kind, I skipped ahead until the illustrations and photographs began. "This is way too complicated for me. Look. They've included samples of the types of cakes you can make with these instructions. Hey, check it out. This one looks like a purse. And that one is a Christmas tree. Wow. I had no idea this edible goop could get so detailed. This guy made an Eiffel Tower. And this one? A perfect replica of an old-fashioned mail box. That's just impressive."

Sighing, since no matter how many pictures I showed the dogs, neither expressed any interest, I skimmed through the pages, looking for anything that could catch my eye. About two-thirds of the way through the book, I caught my breath and stared at my dogs. How the bejeezus do they do it?

Chapter nine dealt with more examples of what one could do when they applied the techniques they learned from this book. This particular section dealt with themed cakes. More specifically, *board games*. There, on the page, complete with board, playing pieces, stacks of cards, and the distinctly colored funny money, was Monopoly. Whoever created the cake even drew a likeness of Uncle Pennybags on the center of the board.

Jillian descended the stairs at that time and saw me sitting in the lounge with a book propped open on my lap. Curiosity had her coming over to my chair to see for herself what I was reading.

"Working with fondant? You want to learn how to decorate cakes?"

"Hardy har, har. Get a load of that."

"Monopoly!" Jillian exclaimed. "I know that's a corgi clue. How did they know to find it in that book?"

I shrugged. "If you ever figure that out, then please clue me in, would you?" I snapped a picture of the specialty cake with my phone.

My wife pulled out her own and waggled it. "Say the word and I'll arrange for all of us to meet for dinner at … no, it's much too late for that. Hmm, we have just one day left. Tell you what. Let's break with tradition and meet for breakfast."

"That works for me, my dear."

"Any place you'd like to go?"

"I'm good with whatever you choose."

My darling wife didn't even wait to see if I meant what I said. She leaned in to give me a kiss on my cheek before she darted away, humming merrily. I looked at the dogs and ruffled each of their fur.

"Didn't really think that through, did I? Wow. The Chateau doesn't serve breakfast, do they?"

TEN

Jillian has got to be, hands down, the most beautiful, wonderful woman in the world. Yes, I may be biased when I say that, but when I placed responsibility for choosing the restaurant to hold our corgi clue review session, I thought for certain she'd choose her favorite, the Chateau. Turns out they do, in fact, serve breakfast. For the record, the menu looked just as horrible as the dinner version. Single-handedly the fanciest restaurant in PV, and pretty much in the entire southern Oregon area, the Chateau's menu was entirely in French. That should give you an idea just how fancy it is. Do I speak the language? I most certainly do not. That is why, during my first visit there, I mistakenly agreed to order frog legs. It was also why I had a teeny, tiny French to English dictionary presently stored in one of my pockets. However, for this particular excursion, it wasn't going to be needed after all.

My lovely wife kept the ruse going until we literally parked on the side of Main Street, directly in front of … Casa de Joe's. I'm sure the relief was evident on my face, because Jillian broke out in laughter as soon as we stepped out of the car. She took my hand in hers and leaned into my shoulder.

"You're welcome."

"I want it known that I didn't request this," I said.

"I know you didn't."

"I was fully prepared to take on the Chateau one more time."

"I know you were, which is why I chose here, instead."

"So, I still get the kudos for being willing to return to Chateau, don't I?"

Jillian laughed. "You *do* know that you aren't eating there tonight, right? I'm not sure it counts if we don't even make it through the door."

"Half kudos?" I suggested.

Jillian giggled and swatted my arm. "We'll see."

"Hey, bro!"

I looked up. Harry was waving us over from the terrace. Looks like our group was large enough to take up the entire outside area. This time, the round tables had been replaced with rectangular ones, and were currently in a U formation, allowing us all to sit together.

"Are we missing anyone?" I asked, as I held the chair for Jillian and helped her scoot it in. I caught sight of Vance glaring at me before his wife, Tori, popped him on the arm. "We've got a good-sized crowd today. Trust me, we're gonna need it. This case is bizarre, so I can use all the help we can get. Harry and Julie? Glad to see you guys.

Vance, you brought the entire family? That's great! Victoria and Tiffany, glad to have you aboard, girls."

Both of Vance's daughters waved at me.

"Dottie isn't here yet," Jillian observed.

I checked my watch. "We still have a few minutes. Was she bringing anyone?"

"I'd like to say yes, but I don't think she will. She and her latest boyfriend broke up a few weeks ago. I keep telling her I'll try to set her up with one of my friends, but she seems determined to tackle the dating scene alone."

"Didn't she say she wanted your help?" I asked, confused. "I swear I heard her say that."

"You did, and she *did* say that. I can only assume she got cold feet, or maybe she's giving up for the time being. Who can say?"

A blue 1967 Corvette Coupe roared up the street, slowing only when it neared. Together, we watched the classic sports car coast into a recently vacated parking spot located conveniently enough next to my Jeep. Dottie exited the car, saw that we were all watching her, and waved enthusiastically. She hurried to the terrace and gave Jillian and me a hug.

"Hi, guys! I'm not too late, am I?"

"Right on time, kiddo," I told her. "Now, let's see. Vance and family?"

"Check," Vance replied, raising a glass of orange juice.

"Harry and Julie?"

"We're here, bro."

"Dottie is here," I said, nodding.

"That I am. Let's get this party started!"

"I also see Taylor. How are things at Farmhouse Bakery?"

A smiling, short-haired blonde woman waved back at me. She was sitting next to Tori and she nodded.

"No arguments, Zack. Hi, Jillian! Quite the contrary, everything is really good. Makes me think that something bad is waiting for me just around the corner."

Taylor has had her own fair share of bad luck with regard to running her bakery, but thankfully, that seems to be a thing of the past. Her shop has, unarguably, the best donuts in town. If you're ever in the area, you need to try her chocolate long johns. They've never been my favorite, but if they all tasted like that, well, I'd have to rethink my choices.

As my gaze traveled around the table, I *did* notice a few empty chairs. My friends, however, hadn't questioned anything. And, for the record, the empty chairs just so happened to be sitting on my right. Why someone hadn't chosen those spots was beyond me. Making sure no one was watching, I quickly sniffed. Nope, no BO, thank you very much.

"Are you going to create that shared photo album, like before?" Harry asked. "It's so much easier than passing around your phone, bro."

I looked at Taylor. "What kind of phone do you have?"

The baker held up her smartphone. "Same as yours, only this one is the latest and greatest!"

I looked at my wife. "Mine's not that old, is it?"

"Zachary, your phone is only a few steps away from being a flip phone."

"Ha, ha. Oh, perfect. Here they come."

Michael Biehn walked up to the gate separating the general public from Casa de Joe's outdoor terrace and held it open. Jennifer and Dash went through first.

"Good morning," Michael announced, as he smiled at our table. "Got room for three more?"

Vance was the only one in on the surprise. No one else knew that I had invited Michael and his family to our gathering. Well, aside from Jillian, that is. Based on the expressions I saw on my friends' faces, my surprise worked like a charm. I made the introductions as our newest arrivals took their seats.

"I gotta admit that I'm curious as hell about this," Michael said, after he and his family placed their drink orders. "We're going to try and solve the clues your dogs have found?"

"That's the plan," Vance said, chuckling.

"How long does it typically take?" Jennifer wanted to know.

Vance, Harry, and I all shrugged, in the exact same manner. Our wives noticed and burst out laughing.

Jennifer smiled. "Let me try again. Have you guys *ever* solved the clues?"

"Sometimes," I admitted, "and that's usually only a few of them. But, what we have recently learned is that each and every one of them are relevant in some fashion. It's up to us to figure out how."

"If you can't solve them, then how do you know you're on the right track?" Michael asked.

"After the fact," Jillian said. "Usually, after the case is closed, we'll all review the case, and that's how we know the clues were accurate. They always tie in. Somehow."

"Always?" Jennifer asked.

"Always," Tori, Vance, and Harry echoed.

Thankfully, our new friends had compatible phones, which allowed me to set up a shared folder for the pictures.

I had to pass Michael's phone to his son in order for him to get it configured correctly. Michael leaned close.

"I'm never going to understand all this technological crap," he confessed. "Every time I start to understand it, something new comes out and changes everything. I had no idea pictures could be shared like this."

"You should," Jennifer argued. "We've done it before, with Dash's birthday pics. It's how I shared them with everyone at the same time."

"Was that when my phone kept telling me that so-and-so liked a picture, or someone left a comment?"

"Exactly."

"Hmmph."

Once everyone had joined up, and could see what I was looking at, we began. At least, that was the plan, until the waiter arrived and took our order. I don't typically eat Mexican food for breakfast, but I will say that Casa de Joe's makes one fantastic breakfast burrito. I just need to remind them to go easy on the spiciness. Bowls of water were placed for the dogs, and two bowls of kibble (seriously, Jillian thought of everything!) were set down next to the water. Once the dogs had finished, they wandered over to Dashiel and flat-out ignored the rest of us.

"Keep an eye on them," Michael instructed. "Stay on the patio."

"I will," the boy promised.

I rubbed my hands together. "All right, is everyone ready? Let's start, shall we?"

"What am I looking at, man?" Harry was the first to ask, as we all opened the shared album and tapped the first picture. "This is a little early for a Halloween party, isn't it?"

"This picture was taken at the comic con," I began.

"The dogs perked up as this thing walked by. I really can't tell you anything specific about it, but it …"

"He's Optimus Prime," Dashiel announced, unable to hide the incredulity in his voice. "He's leader of the Autobots. You know, the Transformers?"

There's nothing quite like the feeling of being ridiculed by a child.

"Okay, yeah, I've seen the movie. Sure. Optimus Prime. Someone spent some time on that outfit."

"What are we supposed to learn from this?" Michael asked.

"And *that* is why we're here," Vance said, taking a sip of his juice.

"This will make sense later?" Michael asked.

"We hope so," Jillian said.

"Ah. Got it."

"The next picture," I said, as I swiped forward, "is … another shot of Optimus. Right. It's about as helpful as the first one. Anyone got anything? No? Right-o. Moving on. We … Tori? What's up?"

"I'm saying this only because I know how obscure some of these corgi clues are, so I have to point out a few things."

"Go ahead, Tor," Vance urged.

Tori was silent for a few moments as she thought of the best way to organize her thoughts. "We know this robot-guy …"

"… Autobot," Dash corrected, without looking up from his staring contest with Sherlock.

Tori smiled at the boy, but Dashiel only had eyes for the dogs.

"Thank you. Now, this Autobot character, we know

he's the leader, so could the clue be about the forces of good? Or evil? I don't know which he is, but if he's a leader, the clue could also refer to someone in charge."

As one, we all turned to Michael's son.

"He's the leader of the good guys. Megatron is a Decepticon. They're bad."

A couple of really rusty wheels started spinning. A long-forgotten jingle popped into my head.

"The Transformers: more than meets the eye!"

Vance grinned. "I've heard that before."

"More than meets the eye," Jillian repeated. "That's part of their theme music?"

"It's their slogan," I corrected. "No, wait. That's not right. Motto? No." I snapped my fingers. "Catchphrase. That was their catchphrase, because of the simple fact they weren't what they seemed."

Now Tori leaned forward. "They weren't what they seemed. I think *that* might be what Sherlock and Watson were trying to tell us. They wanted us to pay attention to their tagline!"

Harry spread his hands wide. "Dude, how does this help us? Are they supposed to be turning into something else?"

"We're going to have to come back to that one," I decided. "Moving on. Next up, we have …"

"My gun," Michael finished for me. He looked up. "This looks like you took a picture of your TV."

I nodded. "That's right. I wanted a clear shot of the gun."

"This isn't a corgi clue?" Jillian asked.

"No, I'm sorry. I guess it isn't."

"Wait, this is what was stolen?" Vance asked. He held

the phone up closer to his face. "What …"

"Put your glasses on," Tori instructed. "That way, you won't have to squint."

Sighing, Vance pulled out a thin pair of wire-rimmed glasses and put them on.

"Just keep the comments to a minimum, huh? Oh, okay. Yeah, I remember this gun. This scene? This is when you were schooling Ripley about how the gun worked?"

Michael nodded. "That's right."

"Can't believe you were in that movie, bro," Harry said. He raised a glass. "Here's to Corporal Hicks, the coolest person we know!"

I lifted my glass. "Lt. Coffey."

Michael gave us all a grin and lifted his own. "Here's to the most interesting convention I've ever attended."

We all heard a loud chirp, as if the world's biggest cricket was sitting under my chair. I checked my phone and saw I had just received a text. It was from Harry.

I CAN'T BELIEVE WE'RE HANGING OUT WITH MICHAEL BIEHN!

WE'RE AT THE SAME TABLE. WHAT ARE YOU TEXTING ME FOR?

I DON'T KNOW, MAN!

GOOFBALL.

"What are we looking at now?" I heard Dottie ask. "This looks like a family that is walking by. Wait. Isn't that …? Weren't you …?"

"I'm going to need you to finish your sentence, Dottie," I teased.

Dottie tapped the table. "You were here, weren't you? There's the tree, and there's the fire hydrant over there. So, what were the dogs looking at? A passing family?"

I shrugged. "I couldn't tell if they were watching the family, or maybe the passing cars. I don't know."

"Does anything stand out to anyone?" Jillian asked.

When no one said anything, I swiped to the next photograph. "Moving on. We … nope. There's another of the family. And yet another. Brother. Okay, here's something new. Looks like we're back at the convention. There are Sherlock and Watson, and it looks like they're playing with some kids."

"When were these taken?" Taylor asked.

I tapped my phone's display and looked at the extra information that my phone embeds into every picture I take.

"According to this, we need to ask Vance that question. He's the one who took it."

Everyone turned to the detective.

"Yeah, I remember taking this, only I don't remember why. Give me a minute. I want to see if it comes back to me."

"What time did they attempt to steal that book?" I asked.

Vance sent off a text message. A few moments later, he received a response. "Just before noon."

"Your picture was taken at 11:58 a.m. Coincidence?"

We all studied the pictures. Sherlock and Watson were frolicking with a group of five or six kids, ranging in age from ten or eleven to at least sixteen. One kid in particular had me paying close attention. After zooming in as much as I could, I studied the older kid who was kneeling next to the dogs. As luck would have it, I had a clear shot of her face, and it was one I was pretty sure I'd seen before.

"Vance? Can you get a copy of Phoenix's mug shot?"

"What? Why?"

Tori smacked him on the arm. "Don't argue. It looks like he's on to something. Get him the picture!"

Grumbling, my detective friend pulled up the picture and fired it off to Jillian in a text message. Moments later, Jillian's phone dinged loudly, like a bell. My wife slid her phone over to me.

"Jillian has it now. What's going on?"

I knew I was right as soon as I saw the photo. In response, I slid my own phone over.

"Check this out. Look at the girl closest to Sherlock. For the rest of you, zoom in on the red-headed girl kneeling next to Sherlock. I do believe she's one of the hobbits. More specifically, the one who's currently locked up."

Vance was on his feet. "Zack, you rock! How in the world did we miss this?"

"I'd say his only job was to distract your dogs," Jennifer said. "You've done your homework. I'd say they've done theirs. They probably knew Sherlock and Watson were there, so they took measures to keep them distracted, only it didn't work."

"This is Phoenix," I muttered, mostly to myself. Then I looked up at the group. "When arrested, *he* was disguised as such, but later we learned *he* was a *she*."

"More than meets the eye," someone said.

Everyone around our table fell silent, including me. Occasional traffic passing in front of us was the only thing that was now heard. Slowly, everyone turned to the speaker.

"Think about it," Tori urged. "More than meets the eye. You all think this Phoenix person is a boy. What if they *all* are girls? Wouldn't that be the ultimate disguise? Letting everyone think they're male?"

That was one way to incorporate the Transformers clue, that's for sure. Personally, I'd have to think about that one some more. Vance, on the other hand, wanted answers. He pulled out his cell and sent off several messages.

"Definitely food for thought," I said. "Let's move to the next picture. Here we have … hmm. I don't know what this one is. Wow. I don't remember taking this one at all."

"That's because I did," Vance clarified. "I was standing with the group of kids dressed as the Avengers. The dogs had just finished playing with those kids from the previous pic when Sherlock started woofing. I didn't know what had caught their attention, so I took a couple of pictures. There, see the bald guy dressed in the red shirt? I remember him. He was a vendor, and he was accusing the girl in the cheerleader getup of stealing."

I studied the photo. The vendor? I didn't recognize him. The girl, however, was a different story. Something about her seemed familiar.

"Zachary, what is it?" Jillian asked me.

"There's something about that girl," I decided. "I can't place my finger on it. She's familiar somehow."

"One of the hobbits?" Jennifer suggested.

"Hmm. I'm not sure. I'm hoping it'll come to me. Let's move on. Great. Another picture of the two of them arguing. Let's see what's next. Okay, moving on. Next up is more girls, only this time they're dressed in uniforms."

"Where was this taken?" Jennifer asked.

"Cookbook Nook," Julie, Tori, and Taylor answered.

"It's my store," Jillian admitted. "Although, I have to say I don't remember these girls there. All right, does anyone have any insight?"

"Zack's a perv?" Harry suggested.

Julie choked on her drink and socked her husband in the gut. "Harrison! Seriously?"

"I was jokin', Jules! I swear!"

"It certainly looks that way," I cut in, hoping to steer Julie and Harry away from a full-blown argument. "I remember these three now. I believe they went upstairs. They weren't there long before heading back down. The dogs were sure interested, though."

"I wonder why," Jillian said, as she studied the picture. "Girls? Sports? Volleyball? Jerseys?"

"What about blonde, or brunette, or African-American?" Tori offered. "That's the three on the stairs. Zack, were there more?"

"Yes, but Sherlock and Watson only watched these three. I have no idea what the other kids were doing."

"You took three pictures of them," Jennifer observed. "And we don't know why. Are you sure this is the way we're supposed to decipher these clues?"

"I know it doesn't look like it," I began, "but these will all make sense soon. There are links here, we just have to find them."

Jennifer shrugged. "Very well, if you say so. Can we go to the next?"

I nodded. "Yes. All right, now you should all be looking at ... board games."

"A whole stack of 'em, bro," Harry said. "What for, man?"

"Which games?" Julie wanted to know.

Collectively, we all zoomed in on the picture.

"I see Risk, Candyland, and Clue," I reported.

"Monopoly is under Clue," Jillian added.

"I count eight games," Tori announced. When everyone gave her a blank look, she shrugged. "Hey, just in case we're not supposed to be looking at which games, but the number of games, I decided to count them."

"Smart thinking, Tori," Vance said. "Board games. The number eight. Is this Woody's place?"

"Yep," I confirmed. I looked at Michael and Jennifer. "It's a toy store in town. It caters to all kinds of hobby enthusiasts."

"After the board games, which I have no clue how they could be pertinent," Vance was saying, "it looks like we have a picture of … this doesn't make sense. Zack, why am I looking at a picture of Officer Riley and his family?"

Jennifer gasped with surprise. "Oh! Look! Do you see what the boy is holding?" She held her phone down low and beckoned her son over. "Dash, what is the little boy holding?"

"A Transformer. That's Bumblebee. He's yellow, and he turns into a beetle."

"A beetle," I repeated. "That definitely confirms those shape-shifting robots are part of this somehow. For the record, I like Tori's deduction. More than meets the eye."

Tori beamed a smile at me while Vance frowned.

"You're just trying to make me look bad."

"Maybe because it's so easy to do?" Jillian teased.

Vance squawked with surprise.

"Moving on," I said, chuckling, "we have a lovely shot of a janitor closet."

"Where was this one taken?" Michael asked.

"Our local police station," I answered. "We were trying to find out how the first hobbit we snagged managed to walk out the front door. In this case, he was dressed like a janitor."

For the next ten minutes, Vance and I described how the station was infiltrated by a second member of the hobbits gang and, moving unnoticed throughout the station, was able to drop a bundle of clothes inside our suspect's cell. Since no one pays attention to the guy pushing the mop bucket, or holding a broom, both suspects waltzed through the front door.

"These guys are ballsy," Michael decided. "Or girls. We don't have any way to know, do we?"

"We know one of them is," I said.

I couldn't have timed it better. Vance's cell suddenly buzzed, indicating the arrival of a text message. "What if Tori's right? What if all the hobbits are girls?"

"I'm starting to lean that way myself," Vance admitted. "Only time will tell, I guess. Is that all of the pictures?"

"There's one more," Jennifer announced. "And it's a picture of a cake that looks like a Monopoly board. Wait, that picture of all the games? Monopoly was there, wasn't it?"

"It was," Jillian confirmed.

We all swiped to the right a few times to scroll backward through the album. Yes, Monopoly was there. But, what did it mean?

Jennifer looked at Tori. "You said there were eight, didn't you? Of those games?"

"I did, yes. The image is a little blurry once you zoom in all the way, but you can still count the individual board games stacked on top of one another, like books. Why?"

"One of the pictures I just passed. Maybe it's a fluke, and I could be grasping at straws, but did anyone else notice one of the volleyball girls wearing a jersey with the number fifty-three on it?"

"How does fifty-three equate to eight?" I asked.

"Duh," Dashiel said, still playing with my dogs. At the moment, both Sherlock and Watson were demonstrating just how well they knew how to shake "Five plus three equals eight. Everyone knows that."

Humiliated by a kid twice in the same evening. That's just swell.

I had a sudden flashback to the kids in Cookbook Nook. As soon as I pulled up the photos, I couldn't help but stare in wonder at my dogs. They did it again. There, on one of the girls' jerseys coming down the stairs was a very noticeable number eight.

"What do you have there, Zachary?" Jillian asked. "Another eight! Jennifer, I think you hit the nail on the head. Somehow, that number plays a part in this."

"The number eight," Michael repeated, unable to hide the skepticism in his voice. "Do we know how?"

"Not yet," I told him. "And the other clue that was repeated? Monopoly was found in the stack of games in Toy Closet, as well as in the cake decorating book in Jillian's store."

Vance snapped his fingers. "The old man."

Most of the table looked at my detective friend.

"What was that?" I asked. "What old man are you talking about?"

"The old dude," Vance insisted. "The one that's on all the Monopoly boards."

"Uncle Pennybags," Jillian said. "What about him?"

"I remember seeing that character walk around at the convention. Then, in that room we searched at the bed and breakfast, we found the costume. That was one of the hobbits!"

I caught sight of Julie. Harry's wife was silent as she studied one of the pictures on her phone. Then, making eye contact with Vance, she indicated she wanted his phone. Curious, he slid his phone over. Julie brought something up on his screen and then did a side-by-side comparison.

"Whatcha got there, Jules?" Harry asked. "What are you lookin' at?"

Julie tapped Vance's phone. "I have Alex's mug shot on this one, and this picture of the cheerleader on mine. See the one where the guy selling comic books was accusing the girl of something? Probably theft?"

"I remember," Vance said, growing interested. "What about it, Jules?"

She spun the two phones around and presented them to Vance. "I think Alex must be short for Alexandra. If you look here, you'll see that he, or make that *she*, is the same person. Same features, same nose, and same forehead."

"They're all girls," Michael said. "I'll be damned."

"And no noticeable Adam's apple."

"That can't be right," Vance insisted. "We apprehended Alex as he left with the book. He was dressed in the long green duster. Zack, didn't you tell me you recognized the character?"

"Data, from *Goonies*," I clarified. That's when it hit me. I slid Julie's phone over and looked at the cheerleader. "That's Andi, also from *Goonies*. Our thieves must've chosen to dress like characters from the movie. Check all the pictures. See if anyone can see any other characters."

"I have no idea what I'm looking for," Vance confessed.

Dottie slid close. "It's one of my favorite movies. Here, I'll help you look."

"*Goonies*," Michael repeated. He looked at Dash. "Son, do you know which movie that is?"

"Kids looking for One-Eyed Willie's treasure."

Michael looked at me and gave me an imploring look.

"He's right," I said. "Great job, kiddo. You know your movies."

"We watch a lot, 'cause my daddy's been in them."

Jillian closed the photo album and went online. She started searching through social media.

"I'm checking the convention's website. People often tag events as they take pictures. We can search through them, too."

"That's a great idea," I said. "I'd still like to know the reference to the number eight."

"Fifty-three is also tied into that clue," Taylor reminded me.

"Fifty-three," I mumbled. "And eight. What …"

"Herbie," Dash interrupted. "You know, the Love Bug?"

Third time's the charm, apparently. Leave it to a kid to fill in the blanks. The Love Bug? A VW Beetle? As in, Bumblebee, the Transformer, who could turn into a … wait for it … a VW Beetle?

"Their vehicle," I said, offering the boy a grin. "They've gotta be driving a Beetle. Bumblebee, from the Transformers, remember?"

"This is great!" Vance exclaimed. He was busy writing notes in his notebook and firing off text messages between writing sessions. "What about fried chicken? What do you think about that?"

I pointed at Dash. "No clue, buddy. You want answers? You should be asking him, not me. He's provided more answers than all of us combined."

Much to his credit, Vance looked at the boy and waited to see if he had an answer. He didn't. Shrugging, Vance returned to his notebook. At that moment, Jillian's cell rang.

"It's the store. I'm sorry, let me step away for just a moment."

I watched my wife step out, onto the sidewalk and wander slowly away as she spoke into the phone.

"I've let the captain know about what we've figured out. He's alerted everyone to be on the lookout for a VW bug that has an out of state license plate. I suggested to him that he should check with the local rental car companies and see if he can determine if any of them rented a VW bug to anyone recently. It's not much to go on, but it's a start."

"And your dogs figured all of this out?" Michael asked, incredulous. "You've no idea how they do it, is that right?"

"No freaking idea, pal," I confirmed. "I wish I did. It could be … hang on. My phone is ringing. Hello? Wait, who's this? You *what?*"

My tone of voice caused everyone in the vicinity to stop what they were doing and stare at me.

"If you so much as … don't tell me to shut up, lady. Yeah, drop the act. I've figured out you are all girls. Yeah, I'm listening. No, I want to talk to her. I … she hung up!"

I was out of my chair and pacing. Sherlock and Watson barked, and not in an excited, happy to see me kind of way.

They both knew something was up.

"What happened, bro?" Harry was asking.

"It's Jillian. They've taken her!"

ELEVEN

ow? How could they have gotten her so easily?"
Vance demanded. "I mean, we were all right there
and she only stepped away for a freakin' phone call!"

"They must've been watching us," I said. Shock had
settled in and I quite honestly didn't know what to do.
These little punks had upped the game, and I had to admit,
were playing it better than me. "What do we do?"

"We've already determined they were behind the phony
call, pretending to be someone at Cookbook Nook," Vance
told me. "How they did it, I don't know."

"Her work phones," I said, groaning. "She bought a
new phone system, one with a ton of bells and whistles.
One of the features is that she can log into the system

remotely. I'd say one of *them* did just that, and spoofed a call from the system. It's the only way I can think of that Jillian's cell would identify the call as coming from Cookbook Nook."

"That really doesn't make me feel any better," Vance admitted.

"Right there with you, pal. You know what this is all about, don't you? This is retaliation." We were back at the police station and I was pacing in front of Vance's office. "I'd say they've been unsuccessful at figuring out how to spring their incarcerated friend, so what do they do? Try and force our hand."

Vance's demeanor sobered and he pointed at his chair. "Do you know what this means? First and foremost, they really want their friend back."

"Obviously."

"If they manage to get their gang back together, then I'd say there's no way we'll ever be able to get our hands on them again. If I was them, and I had this much trouble in one town, I'd cut my losses and just vanish."

"Meaning Michael's gun would remain hidden," I said, "and that they could come back at their leisure to collect it."

"Right."

"So, what do we do?" I asked. "What if they don't call? What if they're doing this just to prove a point?"

Vance ticked off points on his fingers. "First, I believe those kids still think they're smarter than everyone. For whatever reason, they've got this huge chip on their shoulders, and they're desperate to prove to the world they're capable of pulling off a stunt like this."

"That doesn't really help us," I said.

"Second, we've managed to capture two of their gang. Granted, one got away, but we still have one of them."

I started to calm down. Somewhat. "I'm willing to wager *that* wasn't part of their plan."

"Do you know how many cases I've worked that involved more than one person and each of those people couldn't wait for an opportunity to stick a knife in their back?"

"Why do you say that?"

"Because, Zack, I want to know why would this particular gang risk everything to get their missing friend back?"

"Why wouldn't they?" I countered.

"Usually, there are agreed upon actions should things not go their way. If there's too much media attention, or your getaway car breaks down, or any number of other situations, there has to be some type of plan in place. More often than not, it results in all members walking away from the job and going their separate ways. But these guys? Either these people are afraid Phoenix is going to spill the beans on their entire operation, or ...?"

"... or they're refusing to walk away," I finished for him. "Why? What would stop them from, as you put it, cutting their losses?"

Vance's face lit up and he snapped his fingers. "Family. You don't leave family behind." My detective friend grew excited. "What do you want to bet that Phoenix is related to one of the others?"

"How do we verify that?" I asked. "It's not like they've ever been identified."

"Jillian has been taken," Vance reminded me. "Now's the time to pull out all the stops. You and the dogs are very well known. It's time to use every resource at your disposal, pal. So, ask yourself something: is there someone we can call that'll help us positively identify this group once and for all?"

My swirling thoughts latched onto a snippet of conversation I had overheard back when all this mess had started. It was something Julie had said. She told us these guys were known for pulling off daring heists in the United States, yes, but prior to that? They were in Europe. Was that the key? We had to find someone *across the pond* with access to more databases than we had?

Then it clicked. I knew exactly who to call. "Hand me the phone, would you?"

Vance yanked the handset off his desk phone and handed it to me. "Who are you calling?"

"A friend who lives in England. Are you allowed to make international calls here?"

"You'll need an access code to complete the call." Vance pulled out a desk drawer. "I've got one handy."

It took me a few moments of digging through my phone's call history, and my personal email account that, thankfully, my phone was configured to access, before I found it: the personal cell number to one Sergeant Major Davis Forrester. He was someone I met while we were in London, investigating the disappearance of Jillian's brother.

"Hello? Is this Sergeant Major Forrester? I'm so sorry to bug you at this hour. I can only assume it's super late—or early—in England right now. This is Zachary Anderson, owner of a couple of dogs you might remember."

Thankfully, my British friend had already recognized my voice and assured me he remembered me. I filled him in on everything that had happened in the last two days, wrapping up with Jillian's abduction.

"By any chance, Mr. Anderson, do you have their pictures?"

"As a matter of fact, we have the mugshots of two of them. Also, if it helps, we think we might know what kind of car they're driving."

Vance was nodding and flashed me a thumbs-up.

"Go ahead, Mr. Anderson."

"A VW Beetle. I don't have a color, and I don't have a year, unfortunately."

"Then, how could you possibly know one is involved?" Davis asked me.

"You've met my dogs, right?"

"Ah. That I have. Very well, I'll include that in my query."

"I've got both mugshots right here," I confirmed, as I pulled up the pictures in my photo album.

"Do send them to me. We have probably one of the most sophisticated and thorough pieces of facial recognition software available. If records exist for these people, we'll find them. Ah, lovely. I just received your text. Yes, I see them. Leave it to us, my friend. Officially, the Crown is delighted to lend its resources to you. As a personal favor, I will inform you the moment we have anything."

"I definitely owe him a beer," I said to Vance, after I hung up the phone and relayed what I was told.

"Awesome news, pal," Vance told me. "See? We'll get some answers yet."

Several minutes passed in awkward silence.

"If they so much as hurt her," I began, "then I'm ..."

"... gonna have to wait in line," Vance finished for

me. "Those kids screwed up by taking her. Captain Nelson has sent out a public alert. Jillian is probably the most recognizable and loved citizen in PV. We now have about three thousand sets of eyes looking for her. We've also notified Medford and the surrounding areas. If they're out there, it won't take long to find them."

"Don't you think they'd know that?" I pointed out. "Honestly? I can't figure out what their reasoning is here. These people are smart. Aren't they going to know that we'd take this matter straight to the public? This is such a small town. I would think they'd know they wouldn't be able to show their faces anywhere."

"They're immature," Vance decided. "That much is clear. We have one of them, so what's the logical choice? They take one of ours. I honestly don't know how they think they're going to pull off an exchange and make a clean escape. Honestly, I thought they were desperate to prove they're smarter than everyone else. All this does is prove they're desperate, all right, but not to show how smart they are. No, they want their friend back. So, what we need to be doing right about now is …"

My cell rang. Looking at the display, I saw an unfamiliar number that started with a *44*. I held my breath and looked at Vance.

"It's a call from the UK. That was quicker than I thought. Fingers crossed. Davis? Tell me you've got some good news for us."

"And here I thought you were presenting me with a difficult task," Davis's voice announced. "We have identified your two thieves. Once we had their names, the rest of their files didn't take long to find."

"You found them!" I exclaimed. Vance and I gave each

other a well-deserved high-five. "I'm putting this call on speaker. I've got a friend of mine here with me. Vance, this is Davis Forrester. Davis, please meet Vance Samuelson, Senior Detective of the Pomme Valley police."

"Pleased to make your acquaintance," Davis stated.

"And yours," Vance returned. "Whatcha got for us?"

"Your friend? You said she called herself Phoenix?"

I leaned forward. "That's right."

"Her real name is Fenisia O'Connor. She sometimes goes by Fenix, but spelled with an F, and not a P. Fenix and her sister, Charlene, have quite a long list of infractions including, and certainly not limited to, breaking and entering, petty theft, and grand theft auto."

"Charlene," I repeated. "Let me guess. Goes by Charlie, right?"

We heard some papers shuffling. "That's right. Charlie might be the younger sister, but she is more of the risk-taker. Whatever she was involved with would inevitably include Fenisia."

"They're all girls," Vance said, thinking aloud. "Zack had this one pegged earlier. He just knew there was more than meets the eye with this case."

I gave my friend an incredulous stare. "Let's focus on getting Jillian back, shall we? We can laugh and joke about this later. I just want my wife back."

"I might be able to help you with that, too. And, once more, I take my hat off to your dogs."

"The car," I breathed. "You found someone who has a Beetle?"

"Listen to this," Davis instructed. "The O'Connor sisters have records. This is known. What is also known is that they have several known accomplices, two of which are first cousins: Alexandra Reynolds and Danielle Hopkins."

"Dani with an *i*," Vance breathed. "Damn, Zack, you are two for two! Danny is Danielle. Who would've known?"

"No one, unless someone ran a DNA profile on them," I said.

"Or get themselves hurt and are admitted to a hospital," Davis added. "Doctors are bound to notice a few things, aren't they? Anyway, we checked for last known locations. Of interest was one Sebastian Reynolds, great-uncle to Alexandra. According to the records, he lives in Anchorage."

"Great city," I said, shrugging. "Alaska is a long way from here."

There was a pause on the phone.

"It says here Mr. Sebastian Reynolds doesn't live in Alaska. No, this Anchorage is in the state of Kentucky."

Everyone fell silent.

"Fried chicken," Vance stated loudly.

"What was that?" Davis asked.

"One of the dogs' clues," I said. "They homed in on fried chicken. We didn't know which chain of fried chicken stores they meant. Damn. Should've known it'd be *the* fried chicken restaurant. I never knew there was an Anchorage in Kentucky. So, if the dogs clued in on this guy, do we know why? Why'd his name come up?"

"Mr. Reynolds has two vehicles registered to his name," Davis explained. "The first is a 2017 Toyota Highlander SUV. The other, a 2015 VW Beetle."

Davis then gave us the vehicle's license plate number and color.

Vance let out an exclamation of triumph. "That's it! Way to go Sherlock and Watson!"

"Mr. Anderson," Davis continued, "are your wonderful dogs with you right now?"

"They most certainly are," I said. "Vance? Where you are going?"

"I'm letting the captain know. He's going to want to get moving on this just as soon as possible."

"If you don't mind me asking," Davis said, "may I inquire how your dogs indicated that particular make and model of vehicle was involved in your case?"

"The number eight."

"I'm sorry? Did you say …?"

"The number eight," I repeated. "Ever see the Disney movie *Love Bug?*"

"I have. What does that have to do with it?"

"What number is on the hood of the car?"

"Fifty-three, if memory serves. Oh, heavens above. Five and three is eight, is that it?"

I thanked my British friend for his help and hung up. I went to look for Vance, but before I could make it out of his office, my cell rang. Looking at the number, I could tell it was from Pomme Valley, but not on my contact list.

"Hello?"

"Mr. Zachary Anderson. It's so good to finally meet you."

The blood drained from my face the moment I heard the distorted voice on the line. My breath caught in my throat. "You've got my wife. You wanted my attention. Well, you've got it. What do you want?"

"Exactly what you think we want," the heavily disguised voice informed me. "Your wife for our colleague."

Where was Vance? I started for the door.

"Stay in the office," the voice snapped. "You'll move

when I tell you to move."

They knew I was in Vance's office? That could only mean ...

"Yes, we're watching you," the kidnapper confirmed, "so no screwing around. You'll do exactly as we say if you ever want to see your wife again."

I gritted my teeth.

"What do you want me to do?"

"The first thing you're going to do is lock those insufferable dogs in the office. Once you do, head toward the station's front entrance. You will stay on your phone as you go. Go now. There is no one looking. It's time for us to start our own little adventure, don't you think?"

Sighing, I stood. I had no idea what they were planning. They had to know I couldn't bust out their friend, right?

"Sherlock? Watson? Stay here. I've got errands."

Sherlock's head lifted from the floor. He eyed me, then the phone I was holding, and then turned to his packmate. Without warning, both of them started barking their fool heads off. Ever hear a dog barking inside a building? It felt like my eardrums were going to rupture.

"What are they doing?" the voice hissed on the phone. "Make them stop! Hurry!"

No matter how hard I tried, neither dog paid any attention to me. They didn't stop until Vance and a bunch of other cops came running up to me.

"What is it?" Vance demanded. "What ...?"

My detective friend saw my ashen complexion and noticed I was on the phone. He grabbed it out of my hand and put it on speaker.

"What do you want?" Vance asked.

"Prisoner exchange. Our friend for his wife."

Vance automatically looked over to see Captain Nelson staring at him. He immediately nodded.

"Fine. You win. Where and when?"

"Put Mr. Anderson back on the phone," the voice demanded.

"I'm here," I said, leaning over the desk.

"Take it off speakerphone and pick up your cell. Now, you'll do exactly as I ... *what did you do?*"

Confused, I looked at Vance. "What are you talking about? I haven't done anything. Why?"

Vance held a finger to his lips and pointed at the captain, who was holding a black AC power adapter in his hands and giving me a silent nod. He had cut power to their modem and kicked the hacker out of the department network!

"Tell me where to get my wife," I pleaded, as I returned the call to the speakerphone.

"Like we can trust you."

"You want your friend back, don't you?" I countered. "Obviously, I want my wife back. We'll make the exchange. When you four are back together, you clear out of town. What do you say?"

Ten seconds ticked by. "There's a farm outside of town. Highway 238 and Rossanley Drive. Be there in ten minutes, and you'd better come alone or else we'll disappear, you got that?"

"I'll be there."

The call went dead. Several officers appeared, holding onto the arms of one shackled Hobbit of Highton. Phoenix, or should I say *Fenix*, smirked at me, as though this was part of their plan from day one. Then again, who knows? It might have been.

Vance tossed me a set of keys. "Squad car five. It's parked right outside. Take it and her and just go."

"Why can't I take my Jeep?"

Vance pointed at the prisoner. "If you did, then you'll have no way to restrain her. Can't have that, can we, Fenisia?"

The girl glared at my friend. "How do you know that name? I go by *Phoenix*."

Vance motioned for the two officers to bring the girl along. Together, the five of them made their way to the front entrance. Everywhere I looked, police officers were gathering their gear and rushing for the door. The captain wasn't taking any chances with Jillian's life.

My phone suddenly chirped. Pulling it out, I found a message from the captain, only it seemed to be addressed to more than one person. I would later learn that he had sent out a group text message to everyone in the department. I was instructed to play along and maintain the illusion that we were all headed out. He also mentioned that he and the dogs were going to follow from a safe distance.

The captain was going to follow? And he's bringing my dogs? What in the world was going on?

I was led to the waiting squad car. Fenisia was secured in the back as I slid behind the wheel. I've never driven a police car before and, frankly, I was surprised that they'd willingly give me the keys to this one. Since when do civilians drive police cars to a hostage exchange? Something wasn't making any sense here.

Pushing my misgivings aside, I had to focus. I had to think of Jillian. I started up the squad car. It really wasn't that bad. I just had to ignore all the optional extras that were scattered across the dashboard. And the locked shotgun mounted next to the laptop.

Vance reached inside and pulled the power cord from the small camera hanging below the rearview mirror, turned to look at me, and gave me an encouraging smile. Then, he did something that totally surprised me.

He reached around the steering column and shut off the car.

"Okay, I think that ought to do it. We should be truly alone."

"What are you doing? Don't I have to get going?"

"No," Vance said, shaking his head. He opened the passenger door and helped lift the dogs into the car. "Haven't you figured it out yet?"

"What?" I demanded. "Vance, I don't have time for this. I've got to go help Jillian!"

"We all are," Vance announced. "But first, we make sure they're not watching. That's why we had to get out of the station."

"Didn't the captain already take down your internet?"

"He did, and that was his idea. There's a second connection, used solely by our backup systems. Our data is encrypted and sent offsite for storage. If they got in our primary network, then it's not too hard to imagine they could find the secondary connection and exploit it. Oh, what's the matter, Fenny? Didn't think we'd figure it out?"

The young woman seethed in anger behind me, her breathing a ragged hiss. Sherlock whined once. I gotta tell you, seeing a member of the gang responsible for kidnapping my wife that angry was therapeutic to say the least.

"You've got something up your sleeve," I accused, rounding on Vance. "Care to share?"

My detective friend nodded. "Yep. Watch this. Okay, Sunshine, back on your feet. Let's go."

"Where are you taking me?" Fenisia demanded.

"Back to your cell, where else?"

"But … you're supposed to exchange me for your friend's wife!"

"Oh, we're going to get her back, all right," Vance vowed. "And you? What are you worried about? We're only hicks, right? Aren't you supposed to be smarter than us?"

"You have no idea who you're messing with," Fenisia spat. "We've pulled off heists far greater than this. We've outsmarted everyone. You're no different."

Vance pulled the girl out of the car and led her back to the station.

"Mm-hmm. I'm sure you did." Two police officers appeared out of nowhere. "She's all yours. Zack, where's your Jeep?"

"Dude, I'm so confused."

"We're getting Jillian back, but we can't do it from a squad car. We're taking your Jeep."

"But, you just said …?"

"I know what I said. I'm also pretty sure we were being watched at the time. As much as I'd like to keep to our original plan, we have to assume they know all about it by now."

I was out of the squad car in a flash. Sherlock and Watson executed Superman leaps out of the car and pulled me all the way to my vehicle. Once inside, I actually peeled out—in front of the police station, no less—as we headed toward Main Street.

"What's the plan?" I asked. "Am I heading for that farm?"

"There's no point," Vance said. "Medford has an undercover officer watching."

"How? How'd they get there so quick?"

"The whole damn area is looking for Jillian, Zack. Practically every cop living in this part of the state is helping us right now. And, it didn't hurt that Captain Nelson was on the phone with Captain Ryerson at the time your call came in. He overheard the last part of your conversation."

"Where am I going? How does this help us get Jillian back?"

"The captain is convinced they're going to bust out Fenisia."

"What? How do they know she's there?"

"Because, they're still in the system," Vance said. "We might not have world-class hackers on staff, but our IT is pretty good. After Alex escaped, we did a thorough search of the entire station. They found two hidden cameras, placed by our thieves when they were janitors."

"You guys left them there," I guessed.

"That's when we knew they were planning on betraying us. I'm guessing they're planning on using Jillian as insurance, to make sure they make a clean getaway, and are going to use those cameras to verify the station is essentially empty."

"So, if they try and show up at the station to get their friend?"

"They're going to be surprised to see that every door is covered. Every vantage point is being watched."

"What about Jillian?"

"It's what you told me about before," Vance said. "All the clues must be interpreted. Well, as I understand it, right now, we have one left to figure out."

A light clicked on.

"Monopoly. You think this has to do with where to find them?"

"Head downtown. We're going to canvas Main Street, as well as Oregon and Third through Sixth Streets. In the meantime, you and I? We need to start checking street names."

"That's your plan? Look for anything that resembles a property from Monopoly?"

"It might not be the best, but it's the only lead we have. Now, *think*. Are there any streets in PV that are used on that game board?"

"None that I can think of." I pulled over to the side of the road. "You drive. I need to talk to the dogs."

We quickly changed seats. Once we were moving, I turned to regard my two corgis.

"Okay, guys. We've got a problem. They've got Jillian. They're planning on breaking their buddy out of jail and making a break for it. If we don't do something, then they're going to take Jillian with them. We cannot let that happen. Work your magic, guys. In the meantime, I need to talk to someone who knows this town better than me."

"Who?" Vance asked.

I held up my phone, indicating a call had been placed. "Mayor Campbell? I am so sorry to bother you. This is Zack Anderson. I … you what? You know? How in the …? Never mind. I need your help. You know this town better than I do. I'm looking for any street name that might also be in the Monopoly game. Yes, I know it sounds crazy, but it's something we think Sherlock and Watson are trying to tell us."

"Is she still talking?" Vance quietly mouthed.

I muted the call. "She's thinking."

Vance made it to the end of Main and turned left, onto Sixth Street.

"There are no streets I'm familiar with," the mayor informed me.

"Damn. Well, it was worth a shot. Thank you for …"

"You didn't let me finish, Mr. Anderson. Does the name have to be a street? I can think of a Monopoly reference off the top of my head. Maybe that's what you're searching for?"

"Let's hear it."

"There's a hotel next to the post office. Perhaps you've heard of it?"

"What's the name?" I asked.

"The Park Place Inn."

TWELVE

How are we going to handle this?" I asked. "Will there be enough backup? Are you going to go in there, guns blazing?"

"We don't even know if they're there," Vance pointed out. "Once we know she's there, *that's* when I'll call it in."

We were only moments away from the post office. How could I have forgotten about the Park Place Inn? I've picked up family members who have stayed there before. Talk about the mother of all brain farts. This *had* to be where they were holding Jillian. I felt my breath coming in ragged gasps and ordered myself to calm down. I, for one, couldn't wait to wipe the smirk off those hobbit faces.

"Here we are," Vance whispered, as though we were

worried about being overheard.

The Park Place Inn was a two-story building with thirty rooms, fifteen on each floor. It was laid out in an L shape, with ten units on each floor, facing the street.

There really wasn't any way we could approach in stealth, since the hotel sat fairly close to the street. Every room had windows facing outward, and most of them had their curtains drawn back. Maybe this wasn't the place?

"Woof!"

Vance and I turned to look at Sherlock. My tri-colored corgi was standing on his squat hind legs and looking out the passenger side window. Vance nudged my arm and pointed.

"Look at that!"

A VW Beetle was parked in front of one of the rooms. I kept my eyes straight ahead while Vance pulled into the guest check-in spot under the covered parking by the front entrance. Once parked, Vance was on his phone, relaying what we were seeing. After a few moments, he slipped outside and headed to the lobby, presumably to verify which room they were in.

Every fiber in my being was telling me to rush to my wife's defense. I've always considered myself a very chivalrous person, but I'm telling you right now, if one of the girls responsible for Jillian's abduction happens to show up in front of me, then I'm personally gonna drop kick them into next week. Don't think I won't do it.

"Awwoooo!" Sherlock howled.

"I know, pal," I told the corgi. "I'm pretty sure she's in there. We have to wait for reinforcements, buddy."

"Ooooo!" Watson added.

"Keep it down," I snapped, and immediately regretted

it. "I'm sorry, Watson. I'm not mad at you. I'm just worried."

Never one to hold a grudge, Watson squirmed in place as she tried to give my hand corgi kisses. The three of us waited in silence for what felt like an eternity. In reality, I'm sure it wasn't more than a minute or two.

The police arrived on scene in less than four minutes. It was yet another advantage to living in a small town, and being only moments away from the police station. Five squad cars, two firetrucks, and one ambulance crowded into the hotel's parking lot. Vance emerged from the hotel's front entrance, held up a hand to me—indicating I was to wait—and hurried to join the new arrivals.

Police officers, most of whom I personally knew, streamed out of their cars. Kevlar vests were strapped in place. Weapons were checked, loaded, and slid into their holsters. My detective friend joined the small group and huddled close together, no doubt finalizing their plans to storm the room.

I watched Vance point to the room closest to the Beetle and, silently, the men spread out. Two disappeared into a hallway which, I'm guessing, led to the other side of the building. Vance eyed his companions, nodded once, and then banged on the door.

"Police! Open the door, now!"

Naturally, there was no answer. Vance stepped aside, replaced by an officer holding a heavy, iron ram. He smashed the door open. I held my breath as a stream of people entered the room. I heard multiple shouts, but thankfully, no gunshots. Vance appeared moments later and looked straight at me. He gave me a thumbs-up and waved me over.

Jillian appeared. The new cop I met earlier, Officer

Mason Riley, was in the process of cutting the ropes binding my wife's hands behind her. He gently loosened the gag in her mouth before stepping back. By that time, I had made it to her side.

"Jillian? Tell me you're okay!"

My wife took my hands and gave them a friendly squeeze. "I'm alright. I haven't been hurt."

"Where are they?" Vance asked, as he pushed his way through the small crowd that had gathered around us. "Which way did they go?"

"There was only one of them," Jillian reported. "Alexandra Reynolds."

"She told you her name?" I asked.

"No, but if she doesn't want me to know who she really is, then she shouldn't take calls on speaker. Are you sure you didn't see her? She left only a few moments before you guys broke through the door. I can only assume she knew you were out there, although I certainly didn't hear anything."

"We didn't see her," Vance confirmed.

I thought back to Sherlock and Watson. They had started howling not long after we arrived. Were they alerting us that one of them was trying to escape?

Vance noticed my darkening expression. "Zack, what's the matter? You should be happy Jillian is back, and that she's safe."

"Oh, trust me, I am. However, don't you remember what the dogs were doing in the car? They were howling!"

My friend's eyes widened. "They were, weren't they?"

A paramedic appeared and guided Jillian toward the waiting ambulance.

"Mrs. Anderson, we need to make sure you're okay, so

if you'd be so kind?"

Jillian looked at me and correctly guessed what I was thinking. "Go. I'll be just fine here. There's a better than average chance Sherlock and Watson can catch up to Alex, but only if you hurry!"

I gave her a kiss as I hurried by her. Vance and I sprinted for the Jeep. I was about to jump behind the wheel when I noticed the dogs were still staring out the window. Was that the direction they wanted me to go? Or … did that mean Alex was still close by, and she was watching us?

"Change of plans," I said, as I leapt out of the car, grabbing the dogs' leashes. "I think she's close."

Vance quickly joined me. He scanned the surrounding environment and leaned close. "Which way?"

It was as if the dogs were waiting for that exact phrase. They were off, pulling so hard that I thought they were going to make themselves pass out. Vance fell into step behind me.

"They want us to run!" I exclaimed, breaking into a jog.

It became painfully clear that, in this group, I was the weakest link.

The four of us sprinted toward Main Street. People dodged out of the way. Sherlock, leading our procession, turned left, onto Main. We made it another fifty feet when I noticed someone speed-walking in the distance. This figure was wearing a white sweatshirt and ripped black jeans. It had to be Alex! She stopped at a community bulletin board, but I knew the only reason was to see if anyone was following her. Sure enough, she spotted the dogs and hurried away as fast as she could, without breaking into a run.

"That's her!" I wheezed out. "White hoodie, black

pants! S-see her?"

I'm ashamed to say that Vance practically *flew* by me as if I was standing still. He rapidly shortened the distance between the two of them in record time. Alex saw Vance closing the gap and dropped all pretenses of trying to blend in. She began a pell-mell sprint in the opposite direction, using a combination of parkour moves and any obstacle she could find in the hopes that it'd slow Vance down.

Not a chance. He even had the gall to pull out his phone and report his current whereabouts, all without breaking a sweat or losing any ground whatsoever. Alex let out a cry of dismay and darted across the road, narrowly avoiding being hit by passing cars.

She didn't make it far.

You may recall me mentioning earlier that, thanks to this being such a small town, the police had responded in record time to aid in Jillian's rescue. Unfortunately for the poor young thief, that meant the police were using shortcuts and alleys an outsider would not know. They had her surrounded.

She let out a very unladylike exclamation and tried to escape into the crowds, but she collided with one of the folding billboards prevalent along the busy sidewalk and went down. Hard. Vance arrived a split second later.

"Hello there. We've been looking for you, Alexandra."

"Get your hands off me!" the girl raged. "This isn't possible! There's no way you could have found us a second time! I ... no. No! They're the reason? But, how?"

Sherlock, Watson, and I arrived at that time. The dogs were fine, Vance was fine, but me? I wouldn't be carrying on conversation until my lungs caught up with me. And Vance? He wasn't even breathing heavy.

Jerk.

Police cars materialized out of nowhere. They even temporarily shut down Main while they took the very uncooperative thief into custody. Vance approached and gave me a concerned look.

"Are you okay?"

I held up a finger. "Give me a sec. I'm trying not to puke."

"Did you, or did you not, install a gym in your big, fancy new house?"

"Bite me. Where's Jillian?"

Vance held up his phone. "She's at the station, giving her statement. I assume you're headed over there, right? It'll give you time to catch your breath."

I glared at my friend, seeing how I couldn't tell if he was being facetious or not. Whatever. He was right. I'd like to be able to tell my wife how concerned I was and not sound like an overweight tub of lard, thank you very much.

When you're a part of a police chase in a small town like PV, people are bound to notice. That was why Pomme Valley citizens came pouring out of their businesses, houses, and even cars, as we slowly walked back to the police station.

"Tell me she's safe!" one woman shouted. Turning, I saw Hannah Bloom hurrying across the street. She practically threw herself into my arms. "Please tell me you found her."

"We did," I confirmed.

Jillian's friend sobbed onto my shoulder. "I was so worried!"

"That makes two of us, but it's all over now. Would you do me a favor and let everyone know?"

Hannah's phone appeared in her hand. "Of course. Thank you so much for telling me, Zack."

I pointed at Vance. "Thank him. He's the one who chased down one of the group and caught her. And the corgis? They're the ones responsible for finding her."

Hannah dropped to her knees and hugged the dogs.

We turned on Fourth and slowly trudged north. I think we were going that slowly only because Vance was concerned about me. Whatever. There, the road ended and we turned again on E Street. The police station was on the left, and the courthouse was on the right. More people were here, too. I found out later that the station received no fewer than a hundred calls, all claiming that they knew something about my wife's disappearance. Did any of them pan out? No. And from what I was later told, many of the tipsters paid the station a visit when it looked as though their unconfirmed reports went unheeded. But, that *did* confirm the entire town was looking for her, which made me smile.

Several construction workers crossed the street, on their way to the courthouse. One of them looked our way, nudged the other, and then pointed at the dogs. Both grinned and gave us a wave before they disappeared into the courthouse.

I gave a gentle tug on their leashes to let the dogs know we were moving again and followed Vance toward the police station.

"Zachary!" Jillian exclaimed, as soon we walked into the interrogation room. "Oh, I'm so glad you're here."

"Right back at you, my dear."

"Did you find Alexandra?"

I turned to point at the open doorway. Vance had just walked by, followed by Officers Riley and Jones, holding a struggling Alexandra Reynolds between them.

"You caught her! That's wonderful!"

I pointed at the dogs, who hadn't stopped staring at Jillian with unblinking, adoring eyes. "Thank them, not me. They started woofing as soon as we pulled up. I should have known there was more to it. Thankfully, Vance is in much better shape than me. Alexandra tried to outrun him, but she couldn't do it."

Vance appeared a few moments later. He pulled out the chair next to Jillian and sat down.

"Very glad to see you're safe. You had me worried."

Jillian leaned on Vance's shoulder and nodded. "I know. Thank you. And I'm sorry. I should've known something wasn't right with that phone call. I never dreamed that someone could hack my phone system and make a fake call. I am so sorry to have put everyone through that."

"Hey, it wasn't your fault," I scolded. "Don't apologize for something that you didn't cause. This is on them, and I, for one, will sleep like a baby once all four of them are caught."

"What about the other two?" Jillian asked. "Charlene and Danielle? Do we know what happened to them?"

"They never showed up here," Vance said. "We had all exits covered. We were waiting for someone—anyone—to show up, but no one ever did. I guess they were on to us after all?"

"They had to have known it was a trap," I theorized. "They were probably watching and weren't fooled. Or, perhaps they left more cameras in the station that weren't found?"

Vance shrugged. "Anything's possible. We've got a crew currently searching the building now. We've borrowed some gear from Medford. Apparently, this tech can detect hidden cameras, so hopefully they'll find everything. Zack, what are the dogs looking at?"

Jillian and I looked down at the dogs. Sherlock and Watson were looking at the wall on our right, the same wall that held the one-way mirror in the observation room.

"Is someone in there?" Jillian asked.

Vance rose to his feet and left the room. He was back moments later and shook his head.

"Nope, no one. Let them lead for a bit, would you? No, Jillian, stay put."

"Do you really think the last two members are in the building?"

"We have two of them in custody," Vance reminded her. He beckoned for me to follow. "I'm not taking any chances. Jonesy, would you keep an eye on her for me? We need to check something out."

Giving the dogs some slack, I let them guide us out of the room, back through the bustling station, and toward the front entrance. We were met by two guys wearing dark clothes and identical aviator sunglasses. They flashed badges at us and were about to introduce themselves when they noticed the dogs.

"Well, would you get a load of that? By any chance are those two Sherlock and Watson?"

Vance nodded. "They are. Could you give us a minute? I'm terribly sorry, but we need to ... by any chance are you from Nevada?"

The first man, a short middle-aged fellow with spiky gray hair, held out a hand. He was wearing a light black jacket, a navy-blue collared shirt, and black pants.

"Detective Aaron Smyth, Henderson PD. This is Detective Stan Wentford. We're here to …"

Vance held up his hands in a time-out gesture. "You guys are here for the Hobbits of Highton, is that it?"

Smyth nodded. "You reported you captured one of them? That's why we're here. He's got a lot of things to answer for."

"She," I corrected. "They're all females, FYI. And we currently have two. There's also a chance we could get the other two, so if you don't mind …?"

Vance suddenly smiled. "Detectives, would you care to give us a hand? Zack is right. There are two others out there, and I think the dogs might be on their trail."

"I thought you'd never ask," Wentford said. He gave his companion a slap on the back. "What do you need us to do?"

"Armed?" Vance asked, as we hurried to the door. The Nevada cops fell in step behind us.

"Of course," Smyth answered. "Where are we headed?"

I pointed at the dogs. "Don't know yet. But, they do. Shall we?"

Sherlock and Watson ignored the fact that there were now two strangers following close behind us. They immediately took us across Fourth, heading toward the courthouse.

"Good God, more running," I groaned.

Vance looked over at me. "If you need to hang back, that's fine, pal. Just give me their leashes."

"No, I'm good. I can always pass out later. Look, we're heading to the courthouse. That's where those construction guys went."

Vance gave me an incredulous look. "Tell me the last two members weren't disguised as construction workers, and that we didn't let them walk right by us."

"Could you see their faces?" Smyth asked. His hand was resting on the butt of his gun at his hip.

I shook my head. "No. Their hats were tipped low. They had sunglasses on."

Wentford looked at the sky. "How long ago did you see them?"

Vance checked his watch. "This was less than ten minutes ago."

"They could still be here," Smyth said, growing excited. "Is your courthouse typically open on a Sunday?"

"The lobby is," Vance said.

"We're on it."

"Check outside," Vance ordered. "See if there's a crew, or some type of truck out there, would you?"

Wentford nodded and disappeared around the side of the building. The three of us then looked at the dogs. Sherlock and Watson were still watching the front entrance of the courthouse.

"They're in there," I breathed. "Guys? Find them. Find those who took your mom, okay?"

We entered the lobby and eyed the airport-grade metal detector everyone had to pass through in order to go any further. The corgis remained motionless, resembling nothing more than fuzzy statues. The security guard manning the metal detector gave us a quizzical look. His eyes told me he recognized the dogs, but before he could ask a question, Vance held a finger to his lips.

"What are we waiting for?" Smyth whispered.

"I think they're close," I said. "I also think they might've changed their appearance. That's why the dogs haven't budged. I think they're waiting to see what they look like."

Now, to best describe what happened next, I'll simply tell you what it looked like to me, and then explain what really happened, as I learned later. Off to the right were public restrooms. One for men, and one for women. The door for the women's restroom opened up and two teen girls appeared. The first had long blonde hair, worn impossibly straight and even. Her eyes, I could tell even from this distance, were a vivid blue. She was slender, and probably a few inches shorter than Jillian, making her around five foot three or four. She was wearing a midriff-baring yellow top and tight blue leggings.

Her companion had shoulder-length brown hair, which was worn in a high-ponytail. She was looking down at her cell, so I had no idea what color her eyes were. She was curvier than her friend and her outfit was clearly chosen to flaunt her figure. She was wearing a thin white tee and black capris. Sherlock chose that time to yip once, which caused the brown-haired girl to jerk her head up. A look of utter shock appeared on both of their faces.

Then, it clicked. Hide the hair, put a scowl on her face, and dress her in dark, frumpy clothes. It was Danny! Danielle. Both girls cried out in alarm and sprinted for the door. They barely made it outside before a severely confused Wentford made it back to us.

"Was that …?"

"That was them!" Smyth hollered. "Get after them!"

The two girls ran for all they were worth, ducking and weaving around obstacles and people in their path. They quickly ducked into the alley behind the north side of Main. We caught up just in time to see the girls separate. Knowing full well what Vance was going to ask, I handed him Sherlock's leash as we ran. My friend nudged Smyth and veered left. Wentford appeared at my side and, together, we took the right.

"Where does this alley go?" Wentford quietly asked.

"Main Street is just on the other side of these buildings, on the right," I answered. "There are more shops on the left, and practically all of them have doors that lead back here. You see the dumpsters, right? All it would take is for the girls to find a door that's been propped open."

"Man, all of them are open," Wentford complained, as we slowly walked down the alley.

"Watson? What do you think, girl? Which one do we check?"

Watson's nose lifted. Then again, so did ours. We were nearing Marauder's Grill, which thanks to my constant praise, you'll know has the best barbecue in town. Was Watson hungry, or was she telling us to head inside? Maybe the girl was banking on us not being allowed to follow since we had a dog with us?

I scooped up Watson in my arms. Holding her tight, I indicated the back door to the restaurant, which was—as my new friend pointed out—wide open.

"Come on. We have to check this out."

Wentford stuck his head in the door. "Oh, I'm terribly sorry to scare you, ma'am. Did a young girl just come in here through this door? I'm sorry, ma'am, you what? She did? Zack, your dog is amazing. Come on."

The Nevada cop pulled his firearm and advanced into the restaurant. Waiters and cooks stared at us, in awe, as we walked by.

"What's going on?" an older gentleman asked. He saw

Wentford's gun and paled. "Is there a problem? Oh, Mr. Anderson! I didn't see you there."

I held a finger to my lips. "We followed a suspect in here. We're looking for a brown-haired girl. White shirt, black pants. Have you seen her?"

"I haven't, I'm sorry. A family just left. They had two daughters with them. Both of them looked to be in high school."

Wentford raced by, intent on getting to the front of the building as quick as possible.

"Mr. Anderson? Does this have something to do with Jillian? I heard the worst rumor. She was kidnapped?"

"She was, but she's back. And yes, that girl is one of the four responsible."

"Let me go!" a girl's voice suddenly shrieked. "Get your filthy hands off me! Help! Help! I'm being kidnapped!"

I hurried outside. There, in the process of having her hands cuffed behind her back, was a red-haired girl wearing the exact same outfit as we saw earlier. Obviously, it was Danielle, but how in the world did she change her hair color so quickly? Where did she get a wig?

"Hello, Danielle," I said, offering the teenager the most elaborate smile I could muster. "Remember us?"

"What …? I don't know you. I don't know any of you! Help! Someone call the police!"

Wentford pulled the badge from his belt and held it in front of his struggling prisoner. "I *am* the police, sweetheart. Give it a rest, will you? We'll have plenty of time to talk on our way back to Nevada."

The girl's face drained of color. Then, and only then, did she drop the charade. "How did you find me? There's no way you could've known where we were!"

"Let's say I'm a fan of those dogs," Wentford said, keeping his voice calm and neutral.

I held up a finger, and no, it wasn't the middle finger. Get your mind out of the gutter. "That leaves one, doesn't it?"

"You'll never find her," Danielle spat. "She's smarter than all of us, so she's probably …"

"Smarter than the rest of you?" Vance's voice interrupted. He was laughing, so that had to be a good sign.

We all turned to see Vance and Smyth walking our way, with the blonde girl in cuffs.

"And this must be Charlene O'Connor," I said. "How lovely to meet you."

"How did you manage to identify them?" Smyth asked me. "We couldn't get any information on their identities."

"A friend," I answered. "He works for the British government. Danielle? Charlene? That was very convenient of you, pulling off a number of daring heists in the UK. The Crown knows all about you, and was more than happy to pass that information along to us."

"Go to hell," Danielle snarled.

I looked at the blonde girl. She refused to lift her eyes off the ground. "Looking forward to being reunited with Fenisia? She's there, waiting for you."

The girl's head finally lifted. She glared at me until she noticed the dogs.

"Couldn't hide from Sherlock, could you?" I asked.

"He led us to the right store," Vance confirmed, "but we didn't need to catch her. Someone did that for us. Einstein here tried to hide in Hidden Relics & Antiques."

I burst out laughing. "Oh, talk about a poor career

move." I noticed Wentford giving me a blank look. "That store is owned and operated by Burt Johnson. I'm not lying when I say he's the biggest dude I've ever known."

Smyth held a hand high over his head. "He's not kidding. The guy could twist me into a pretzel without breaking a sweat."

The dogs and I stepped out of the way and let the police do their thing. The girls were read their rights and led away, presumably to join their already incarcerated friends.

Nearly an hour later, we were given clearance to head home. By the time we returned to our manor, we saw that we had a welcoming committee waiting for us. Dottie's blue Corvette was parked in the driveway, and the moment my Jeep pulled up, she bolted out of her car.

"Jillian! Omigod, don't do that to me ever again! I was worried sick!"

As if by magic, more cars began arriving at our home. Taylor was the second person to arrive, followed closely by Hannah and her son, Colin. Harry and Julie pulled up not that long after. I parked my Jeep and invited everyone inside.

"I can't believe you went through all of that," Hannah was saying, as we stepped into the grand salon. "To think that …"

"Woof!"

Sherlock's bark, though quiet in volume, had the effect of silencing the entire house. We all turned to look at the tri-colored corgi, but he was paying no attention to any of us. Instead, he was facing the stairs and looking as though he wanted to go down to the ground floor.

"What's with him?" Taylor wanted to know.

Harry looked nervously around the house. "Dude, tell me one of them didn't follow you back here."

"Harrison, all four were captured," Julie reminded him. "There's no one left!"

"That we know about," Harry uttered, under his breath. "Look at Sherlock, bro. Something is eatin' at him."

Harry was right. Sherlock had triggered on something, but what? Was my friend right? Could there be a fifth person out there?

"All right, boy," I told the corgi. "You want to check it out? Let's go check it out, 'kay?"

The dogs pulled me to my feet and, together, all of us headed downstairs. I thought the dogs might want to do a sweep of the entire floor but no, they guided me straight to a storage closet next to the game room. I opened the door and showed Sherlock and Watson what was inside.

"Well, let's see. We have a few folding tables and chairs on the left. We have a vacuum cleaner on the right. Those boxes, there are Christmas decorations …"

"Bro, don't you have a huge garage?" Harry sputtered.

"Don't get me started," I laughed. "Now, on the shelf up there are extra rolls of paper towels for the bar, and over there we have …"

"You have *what?*" Julie asked.

"Board games," I breathed.

Jillian gasped and clutched my hand. "We have Monopoly up there, don't we?"

I took the game down and presented it to the group. Sherlock and Watson followed the game as it was handed off to several people. I took the rectangular box and headed for the closest chair, which prompted the others to do the same.

"Here we go again. Monopoly. I thought we were done with this, but clearly not. What's left?"

"Getting the gun back, man!" Harry said, as though I was a complete dunderhead for not figuring that out on my own.

"Using Monopoly?" I asked, unable to hide my skepticism. "We know it wasn't in their room at the Park Place Inn. It was searched from top to bottom. Nothing else was found."

"There has to be something else," Jillian insisted. "Guys, it's time to put our thinking caps back on. What else could it be?"

"We've already searched through the names of the properties," I reminded everyone. "There's gotta be something else. Maybe … maybe something with the word *chance* in the title?"

Colin looked up. "What about the other stack of cards? What's it called? Community Chest?"

Everyone present, including Colin, reached for their phones. However, no one found anything with chance, or community, or chest for that matter. I heard my wife sigh.

"We must have missed a property. I'll go back through the list."

The basement was silent as Jillian searched for the list of game properties. However, before she could read any of them aloud, I watched her eyes widen with surprise. She began to furiously tap something on her screen. As for me, a fast texter I am *not*. I use one finger only, and can get out a full sentence by the time Jillian types an entire paragraph, using only her two thumbs. Maybe everyone was right and I was getting too old to keep up with the technology?

"I don't believe it," Jillian exclaimed. "Did any of you know that, in the UK, the list of Monopoly properties are completely different?"

That bit of news got me off my chair. I leaned over her shoulder and looked at what she found.

"I had no idea! Do any of them stand out?"

Jillian tapped on the section which specified what the green-titled properties were. Apparently, the UK version of Pennsylvania Avenue had been the one to catch her eye. She made sure I saw the name of the property before holding her phone up.

"One of the green properties is Bond Street."

Harry let out an exclamation of surprise. "Bond Street Pawn!"

I quickly called Vance and filled him in. He assured me he would call the store personally. Thirty minutes. That's all it took to locate the gun. Half an hour after informing Vance about Bond Street Pawn's connection to Monopoly, there was a knock on my door. Neither of the dogs bothered to rouse themselves, by the way. After our discovery in the closet, both had each claimed an arm chair and were preparing to take a nap. Sherlock watched me head up the stairs before sinking off to sleep.

"You did it, pal," Vance proclaimed, nearly an hour later. He handed me a plastic grocery bag that I could see had some type of bulky item in it. "It took longer than I would have liked to get the owner to cooperate, but there you go. One movie prop from what I'm told is one of the best sci-fi sequels around."

I took the bag and fist-bumped my friend. "Nicely done, amigo. I know a certain someone who's gonna be thrilled to get this back. Wait. You've never seen *Aliens*?"

"I haven't. Is Michael still at the convention?"

I checked the time on my phone. "No, they've wrapped things up by now. But, I do know he won't be flying out until tomorrow morning. Hey, plan on being here at seven this evening, okay?"

Vance nodded. "Sure. Got something planned?"

"You can help me officially break in the theater."

My detective friend looked interested. "You mean, no piddly sub-volume audio levels? You're going full blast?"

"Eardrum shattering, knock-the-pictures-off-the-wall audio levels," I promised.

"Sounds like a blast. Er, pun intended. We'll be there."

EPILOGUE

This is, hands down, the coolest room in the whole place," I was told, several hours later. Vance pointed at the bar. "Everything one would need can be found within thirty feet of this spot. You've got your theater right here, your arcade in there, and a bar on that wall there. You've even got a mini kitchen here, complete with fridge, two burner stove, and a sink. Man, it doesn't get any better than this."

My guy friends clustered around me as we sidled up to the bar. Seeing how I was the host, I decided it was up to me to hand out the drinks. From there, we headed for the seats. Plush, reclining armchairs sat in three rows of four. Drink holders were integrated into the chairs, as were hidden speakers and subwoofers.

All the ladies elected to skip the movie presentation and instead, chose to open a few bottles of wine and watch some television in the lounge. I tried to persuade Jillian to join us on the ground floor. I know she enjoys these types of movies as much as I do, but apparently this particular franchise didn't sit well with her, so she opted out.

I had the popcorn cart thingamajig Jillian bought for me going full blast. The smell of hot buttered popcorn permeated the air, and not one of us, I should point out, elected to forgo the tasty snack.

Looking around the room at my circle of friends, I felt happy. Harry was here, along with his oldest kid, Drew. Vance sat next to them, nursing a beer. He was spouting some false story about whipping our butts in Skee-Ball the last time we got together. For the first time ever, I invited Burt Johnson over, too. He may be intimidating as hell, but the six-and-a-half-foot-tall giant was actually very nice, and oddly enough, a little on the introverted side. But, as with most people, once you got to know them a little better, the walls they build around themselves would drop, and they'd let their hair down, so to speak.

Burt was on his third beer. I knew I didn't have to worry. In his hands, those bottles looked like they belonged in a doll house. Three beers to him was probably the equivalent of a few swallows for the rest of us.

Upstairs, Jillian had Tori, Julie, Hannah, Taylor, and Dottie. I knew they were having a good time because every couple of minutes, loud peals of laughter could be heard. That's when I felt a tap on my shoulder.

"Are we gonna get this thing going?" Vance asked.

It was perfect timing. The doorbell rang. This time,

Sherlock and Watson, who had elected to remain upstairs with the ladies, began barking like crazy.

"I'll get it," I said, standing up.

"The wives are closer, bro," Harry pointed out.

"Oh, I know it. I'm thinking that I'll need to ..."

"Zachary?" Jillian called down from the top of the stairs. "There's someone to see you up here."

"Be right there!"

"Hey there, brother," a familiar voice greeted, as I climbed up the stairs. "Got room for one more?"

It was Michael Biehn. I had extended an invitation to him, seeing how the movie I had selected to play this time around was Jim Cameron's *Aliens*. Much to my surprise, Michael accepted, and here he was. Judging from the shocked expression from the ladies, no one knew he was coming.

"Glad to have you, pal. Come on. We're all downstairs."

Talk about leaving a classroom of kids unattended for a few minutes. When the two of us made it to the ground floor, we could see that a very aggressive game of Skee-Ball was happening between Harry and Burt, and it looked as though a new champion was about to be crowned.

Everything came to a screeching halt when we were spotted. My friends were speechless as they stared at the actor. Michael grinned at everyone, wandered over to throw a few balls on a Skee-Ball table, and shook hands with Burt, the one person he had yet to meet.

You've never watched a movie properly until you watch it with someone who had starred in it in the first place. We laughed, cracked jokes, Michael shared stories from the set, and all ended up having a great time. I learned about how Michael was a last-minute replacement for another actor, who had been fired. He told us all about how he almost didn't get his breakthrough role in *Terminator* due to the inability to shake a southern accent he had used for a previous film. But, all good things do come to an end. Before we knew it, the credits were rolling, people were checking their phones, and it was time to head home. But, before anyone could leave and go their separate ways, Michael posed for pictures and even signed a few autographs.

After everyone had left, and it was just myself, Jillian, and Michael. He thanked me personally for returning his gun and promised if we ever happened to be in the same city again that we would, without a doubt, hang out again. Who knew such a famous movie star could be so personable?

With that, Michael patted Sherlock and Watson a final time before he headed for his car. I wrapped my arms around Jillian and we snuggled close.

"Thank you for one of the most exciting weekends of my life. Hanging out with Michael Biehn in our house? That's gotta be one of the coolest things ever."

As always, I was wrong. Several months from now, I was going to witness something that was going to make the news as far away as the east coast.

AUTHOR'S NOTE

Talk about being a nervous wreck. I finished this novel, and was happy with it, then I must've sat back in my chair and second-guessed myself. What if Michael didn't like it? What if he told me that he changed his mind and didn't want to be in the book after all? All these scenarios ran through my head. But, I did agree to send him a first draft copy once I was done so I could get his input.

I was worried about nothing.

He absolutely loved the story. He loved the Easter eggs, as he called them in his Foreword, I managed to sneak into the story. The story about looking for a grave with Michael Biehn? That has to be, hands down, the coolest break-the-ice story I have at my disposal. Who else can open with … I once went to the middle of nowhere, in Arizona, with Michael Biehn with the sole intention of locating—and digging up—a dead guy. Twice.

In case you're wondering just who we were looking for, well, it'd be none other than Ike Clanton, portrayed by Stephen Lang in *Tombstone*. He's the one who, at the end of the movie, rips off his red sash and gallops away from Wyatt Earp and Doc Holliday. The story goes, Ike was shot and killed by a bounty hunter at this particular cabin, and was buried where he fell. Michael and I drove all the way out there and hiked in to find the cabin. However, as I mentioned, neither of us had any business being out in the wilderness like that. We got turned around, didn't have enough water, and I ended up slipping on the rocks—going downhill in sneakers, of all things—and crunched my shoulder good.

That was a lovely phone call to my wife, let me tell you. LOL! But, even so, I went with Michael a second time to search, this time bringing my brother, who had waaayyyy more experience camping than I do. We found the remains of the cabin much quicker, had plenty of time to actually search for the grave, but didn't find anything. Still, it was a lot of fun.

Sorry for rambling. I get asked to relate that story frequently, so it's not like I haven't said it once or twice. Or twenty times.

The Setting History Straight website. Yep, I set it up. Michael gives me stories he'd like to add, and I put 'em up there. If you haven't already, I recommend stopping by. Michael has had an amazing life. I offered to write his autobiography. I think he might be tempted. :)

As with any book I release, I always like to mention this. If you enjoyed the story, please consider leaving a review. The more positive reviews an author receives, the easier the book is to find on sites like Amazon, or Barnes and Noble, or any number of others.

Thanks for reading! Until next time!

J.
July, 2023

BOOKS BY JEFFREY POOLE

Epic Fantasy
BAKKIAN CHRONICLES
The Prophecy
Insurrection
Amulet of Aria
Disneyland Debacle (short story)
Winter Wonderland (short story)

TALES OF LENTARI
Lost City
Something Wyverian This Way Comes
A Portal for Your Thoughts
Thoughts for A Portal
Wizard in the Woods
Close Encounters of the Magical Kind
The Hunt for Red Oskorlisk (short story)
May the Fang Be With You (Pirates trilogy #1)
The Hammer is Strong with This One (Pirates #2)
These are Not the Stones You're Looking For (Pirates #3)
Blast from the Past

DRAGONS OF ANDELA
Harness the Fire
Strike the Spark
Clear the Water*